Praise for the G

"Solid tween appeal."—*The Globe and Mail*

"A pre–Stephen King novel for tween readers."
—BellaOnline.com

"A storyline that fantasy addicts will devour."
—*Montreal Review of Books*

"[An] appealing mix of realism, whimsy, and legend."
—*Booklist*

"Bubbles along at a magical pace . . . creepy enough to cast a spell over anyone who reads it!"—*Resource Links*

"DeMeulemeester has scored big."—*Vancouver Sun*

"Cat is an engaging heroine, and Grimoire has just the right amount of evil."—*January Magazine*

"An entertaining and worthwhile read."—*Kirkus Reviews*

"We simply want to devour more of this author's highly readable and intriguing prose that she has a knack for creating . . . Next installment, please!"
—*CM: Canadian Review of Materials*

The Family Secret
GRIM HILL

Book Four

LINDA DEMEULEMEESTER

Wandering Fox Books
An imprint of Heritage House Publishing Company Ltd.
heritagehouse.ca

LIBRARY AND ARCHIVES CANADA CATALOGUING IN PUBLICATION

DeMeulemeester, Linda, author
The family secret / Linda DeMeulemeester. — First Heritage House edition.

(Grim Hill ; book 4)
Originally published: Montréal : Lobster Press, 2010.
Issued in print and electronic formats. ISBN 978-1-77203-103-4 (paperback).
—ISBN 978-1-77203-104-1- (epub).—ISBN 978-1-77203-105-8 (epdf)

I. Title. II. Series: DeMeulemeester, Linda. Grim Hill ; 4.

PS8607.E58G715 2016 jC813›.6 C2015-906752-9 C2015-906753-7

Cover illustration by John Shroades

The interior of this book was produced on 100% post-consumer recycled paper, processed chlorine free and printed with vegetable-based inks.

We acknowledge the financial support of the Government of Canada through the Canada Book Fund and the Canada Council for the Arts, and the Province of British Columbia through the British Columbia Arts Council and the Book Publishing Tax Credit.

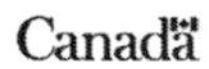

20 19 18 17 16 1 2 3 4 5

Printed in Canada

In memory of my grandmother,
Alice Beatrice Walls (MacPhail),
an amazing storyteller

CHAPTER 1

A SHOCKING ANNOUNCEMENT

It was all too good to be true.

I wondered if my ears were plugged as I said to Mia and Amarjeet, "Did I just hear that right?"

"Cat, shh," Mia rasped. "Ms. Sevren is saying some thing else."

I tilted my head toward the PA speaker as if that would help and listened intently to what our vice-principal was announcing.

"I repeat—this is an amazing opportunity, but because the grant money came in at the last minute, we have only five weeks to organize the school exchange in time for spring break. *Every senior who is interested in participating must meet in the gym immediately.*"

"We've got to get in on this; otherwise, we'll be stuck in this stupid town with nothing to do." Mia slammed her locker door in irritation.

I closed my gaping mouth. Darkmont had no money for any extracurricular activities, not even for any more sports until the next school year, but it just got a grant for a school exchange?

"Where?" I said incredulously. "She didn't say where the exchange was, did she?"

"Does it matter?" Amarjeet threw her own books in the locker, not even caring when they landed open, which wasn't like her. "I'm signing up. Think about it. Most of us aren't even allowed to go into the city with a couple of friends to see a movie. Can you imagine travelling without parents?" Then her face broke out into a huge grin.

"We'll have to be with teachers," I pointed out.

Amarjeet acted like she hadn't heard. "Do you think it will be a big city? I mean, this town doesn't even have a mall."

"Or a rec centre!" This place was so different from my old town. Except for going to the library or the small pool that was only good for teaching little kids how to swim, there weren't a whole lot of activities for the average person. It was early March, and summer seemed like a lifetime away. We *needed* fun!

Zach, Rabinder, and Jasper hurried toward the gym, rushing past us without as much as a "hello." "Hurry," Mia said. "What if it's first-come, first-served? There goes Mitch." Mia pulled off her jacket and, in her rush, twisted it inside out.

As Mia struggled with her sleeves, we ran down the hall, even though we weren't supposed to run, and followed Mitch into the gym.

"Does anybody know where the swap is?" I asked Jasper. Curiosity burned through me.

He shook his head. "No, the only specific thing Ms. Sevren said was that it's for seniors only."

"Well, that's us," I said happily. One good thing about living in this tiny town was that we only had a junior high. All the older kids took school buses into the city. This left us on top of the food chain, even though we were only thirteen.

"Of course there will be other criteria," said Clive, sounding smug as he joined us. "Like good grades." He looked right at me.

"Of course," I said as my heart sank. My grades weren't bad, but they weren't great. And I'd managed to get myself in trouble a few times in school.

"Here we go." Jasper pointed to the stage. Ms. Sevren stepped in front of the shabby velvet curtains, walked on stage, and adjusted the microphone. *Screech*. She tapped the microphone and leaned forward, brushing a strand of steel-grey hair from her eyes.

"Darkmont has the chance to offer our students an incredible opportunity," she began. I couldn't say that was something I heard every day. Then Ms. Sevren got my full attention.

"We are going to do a student exchange with our sister school, Svartberg Academy, in Sweden."

Okay, my ears must have been blocked. Did she say *Sweden*? Mia squealed in delight.

"Our students will have a wonderful opportunity to explore the local museums and galleries and to learn firsthand about the history and geography of the region," said Ms. Sevren.

"Awesome," everyone murmured, though I figured like me, they weren't thinking about the museums at all. Excitement shot through the gym like a bolt of lightning. I could feel the tingling on my skin as I shook my head, dizzy with disbelief.

Travel to Sweden; was she kidding? I'd never been on a plane, and I could barely imagine what it would be like getting out of this town with my friends. Once I'd seen a show that took you on the highest train in the world to a cloud forest in South America. That's the closest I'd ever been to travelling.

"To qualify for this exchange program, Darkmont seniors need to meet the following conditions." Ms. Sevren flashed two sheets of paper in front of us. Everyone stopped jumping up and down on the polished gym floor and stood stock-still.

I held my breath.

"Firstly, you must have a grade point average of B or higher. Even with spring break, participating students will still miss an extra two weeks of school, so you must be in good academic standing."

Done . . . almost. I had a C+ in history, but my science mark was an A-, so it would average out.

"Secondly, although our grant is generous, your parents will still have to cover some of the cost."

My soaring balloon of excitement took a dive bomb. Air hissed between my lips in a sigh. Ever since my parents' divorce, my family didn't have much money to spare.

"But," said Ms. Sevren, "we want to offer this opportunity to as many students as possible. So to qualify for the exchange, everyone must participate in fundraising events over the next four weeks."

Done. My balloon bounced back up.

"Finally," said Ms. Sevren, "you must have your parents sign a letter of permission and the sponsoring teachers, Ms. Dreeble and Mr. Morrows, sign a letter of reference. We will need both in the office by Thursday."

My balloon was now quickly deflating. I wasn't exactly on the good side of either of those teachers. Other students rushed past me to pick up the letters that were now set on a table at the foot of the stage.

"C'mon, Cat," called Amarjeet. "You're signing up, right?"

"Yeah, even you should qualify," Clive said with a wicked grin.

"Guess if they take you, they'll take anybody," I shot back. Clive laughed and nudged me toward the table. When I reached the pile of letters, I still hesitated.

"Don't worry, Cat," Jasper mistook my hesitation; he knew my family didn't have loads of cash. "We'll hold car washes, and I can get my parents to offer a free dinner at their restaurant as a raffle prize. We'll raise a lot of money for the trip."

Jasper Chung was a good friend. But I didn't think he could help me get on the good sides of my teachers. At least, not in two days.

Clive, on the other hand, knew exactly why I hesitated. "Better get that punk hair toned down," he teased, pointing at the green strands in my brown hair. "You know how that annoys Mr. Morrows; it's not exactly in Darkmont's dress code."

That was true. Darkmont was strict about not wearing anything that drew attention, which meant no face piercings, no cool clothes, no distracting jewelry, and no crazy hair. But dye wouldn't work on my hair; once you've been marked by the fairies, there's nothing you can do about it. Somehow, though, I thought Mr. Morrows would be more concerned about a few outstanding assignments I might have forgotten, rather than the colour of my hair.

Also, there was one more thing lurking in the back of my mind. Did I dare wish for anything in this town? It was almost as if a wish could be turned against you here, and it was better to put your heart's desire in a box and lock that box away. Our Valentine's dance had proved that. I shuddered remembering that disaster.

Then it struck me. I wasn't wishing for anything in this town; I was wishing to get *out* of it.

CHAPTER 2
SECOND SIGHT

When I got home, I had the place to myself. It was for the best, because I had to get busy and I didn't need Mom wondering why all of a sudden I had so much homework to do in one night.

I also didn't need my little sister Sookie casting me suspicious glances as I tried to explain my way out of it. I had a lot of work ahead of me if I was going to convince my teachers to sign the reference letter for the student exchange. And I really wanted that trip to Sweden, even though I didn't know much about Scandinavia. But I knew I'd get to fly on a plane, that I'd get to stay in a hotel with all my friends, and that parents wouldn't be with us.

I hauled out my books and got started. Mom had taken Sookie to an eye doctor in the city, and they were going to stay there for dinner. But there was something Sookie had said when she brought home that note from her teacher that had me a little worried.

"My eyes are fine," Sookie had grumbled. "I don't want to go."

"That's not what your teacher says," Mom had explained patiently. "You have a hard time seeing what's been written on the board in your class."

"Oh, I can see the board fine. I just forget sometimes to remember what I'm looking at."

"What on earth do you mean?" Mom had frowned.

But Sookie had only stared at Mom for a few seconds, like she'd been examining a bug on a leaf. I remembered the silence in the kitchen, except for the red clock that had been tick-tocking. Then switching gears, Sookie had asked, "Can we go to the sushi restaurant?"

"Fine by me." Mom had smiled, relieved to have gotten off easy—you didn't want to mess with Sookie when she got into a sulk. Sure, Mom had the upper hand, but it took effort.

I thought about the way Sookie had looked when she'd explained why she didn't need her eyes checked. I realized it was the kind of intense expression I didn't much like, sort of like a cat going after a canary. No, it was more like a cat drooling over a bird through the window.

Suddenly, shivers crawled up my back.

Sookie balanced a regular kid's life with a secret one, and she wasn't old enough to know which secrets were dangerous to keep.

Much later when Sookie and Mom got home, I was still hunched over the computer in the dim light of our study.

"Oh, Cat," Mom said without even a "hello" as she surveyed the oak desk where I'd left an empty popcorn bowl and a plate with cookie crumbs. "Tell me that wasn't your dinner." Mom frowned looking at my dishes.

"I ate a balanced meal," I said. I'd grated cheese on the popcorn, and the cookies had raisins in them.

"So," I asked, looking at my sister, "What's up with that?"

Sookie grumbled. "The doctor said I'm supposed to wear this annoying eye patch at home. Then at school I have to wear stupid glasses," she said, upset enough to use normal third grade talk.

Sookie collapsed in a miserable heap on the stool beside me. She hung her blond head. "Now I see double."

"That shouldn't happen," Mom said as she carried my bowl and plate to the kitchen. "It's supposed to make your weak eye stronger."

"So how many fingers do you see?" I said, holding up one finger.

"One and that's not what I meant." Sookie folded her arms and looked cross.

"What *do* you mean?" I asked.

"Nothing," Sookie said with a hint of mystery. And as soon as Mom disappeared into the kitchen, Sookie pulled off her eye patch. I shrugged and got back to work. Sookie picked up my permission letters and began reading them.

"Hey," I snatched the letters away. "Those aren't yours." In Sweden, I'd be free of my kid sister for three whole weeks.

"Mom," I yelled, "I've got an important paper for you to sign."

"Sookie, put that eye patch back on," Mom insisted when she walked back into the room.

Sookie looked so sad, I added, "You can pretend you're a pirate." She pulled her patch down over her eye and asked, "Can I go, too? I can't wait!"

"Go where?" asked Mom.

I handed the letters to Mom. "Well, you'll be waiting a long time," I said to Sookie. "You're only nine and this is for the eighth graders."

"What's this about?" Mom said, skimming the form.

The letter pretty much explained it all, but Mom liked to hear my take on things. She called it "keeping our communication open."

"There's a student exchange for seniors. Mom, I really want to go. There's a grant and there will be fundraising, and so it shouldn't cost—"

Mom got those lines between her eyebrows as she read—that was never a good sign.

"But I've got to go," I said under my breath, as if saying it too loud would make it not come true—like a birthday wish.

After a minute Mom said, "It would be a wonderful opportunity." She went to the oak desk and opened the drawer, then pulled out a big white envelope. "I have to check these lawyer's papers. I'm sure your father gave permission for you to leave the country . . ." Her voice trailed away. Would Mom need him to sign something?

I'd been about to jump up from the computer and read over Mom's shoulder, but I froze mid-motion. It was as if a fist squeezed my heart. Sookie, who'd been fidgeting on her stool, grew still. We hadn't heard from our father in ages.

Mom forced a smile. "Let me sign your letter, Cat. Don't you worry; I'll work out all the details."

"Thanks, Mom." That moment of tightness passed.

"I can't wait!" squealed Sookie.

"For what? To get rid of your older sister?" I wasn't that bad.

"No." Sookie got that strange look of anticipation on her face again, but she didn't explain herself.

"It's too late to be doing homework." Mom looked at her watch. "What have I said about doing schoolwork after TV?"

Actually, there hadn't been any TV time, or internet time, or any time. I'd been barrelling through schoolwork for hours, and my eyes were getting blurry. "Sorry. I'm almost done."

"Tell your sister goodnight," Mom said to Sookie.

Sookie came over to hug me goodnight, and then she pulled away sharply.

"Cat, watch out for the water!"

"Oops," I said, checking if I had knocked over my glass on the desk. But Mom must have taken that away for me too. "What water?"

"The water, the water . . ." Sookie sounded like she was about to burst into tears.

"Someone sounds very tired," Mom said, ushering Sookie to bed. Maybe I shouldn't have said anything about pirates.

Still, her odd outburst must have spooked me because that night I kept hearing a splash, as if I'd fallen into a pool. I was still sleepy when I woke up. But when I grabbed the letter Mom had signed, and all the assignments to show my teachers, I was wide awake.

Throughout the day I sat through my classes as butterflies tap-danced in my stomach. All the work in my backpack just *had* to convince Mr. Morrows and Ms. Dreeble that I qualified for the exchange.

CHAPTER 3

A DESPERATE ATTEMPT

"Cat, are you going to sign up for the car wash on Saturday?" Zach asked as I passed by my friends in the hall. They'd gathered outside the gym and were organizing sign-up sheets for the fundraising.

Zach was the coolest boy at school, and he was asking me? I signed up for car washing and for the bake sale and for selling raffle tickets.

"Hey, why don't we do a bottle drive and clean up some yards?" I suggested. April was around the corner, and grass would need cutting.

"Great idea," said Zach, and we made up the extra sheets, which I promptly signed.

Amarjeet whistled softly. "Wow, Cat, where are you going to get the time to participate in every single event?"

"I'll have to make time," I said. "Besides, I decided to get a jump-start on homework." I hauled my heavy backpack off the chipped linoleum floor. "And I'm going to hand in a few assignments now, so if you think of any other fundraisers, sign me up."

"Will do," Mitch said cheerfully. Then he joined the current debate: What would raise more money, holding another car wash or another bake sale?

"Cars get dirty every week," argued Amarjeet.

"But people can never eat enough cupcakes," said Mitch.

I left them to decide and went to Ms. Dreeble's class first. The stools had been placed on top of the crowded tables, and I bumped one with my bulging backpack. The stool crashed down, knocking over a Bunsen burner. Ms. Dreeble jumped and turned quickly from the notes she'd been making on the board. Not the best start.

Picking up the stool, I said to my teacher, "I brought you the work I've been behind on."

"What a coincidence," said Ms. Dreeble. "I don't suppose this has anything to do with the exchange trip?"

"It has everything to do with the trip," I said in surprise. *No point in hiding it*, I thought. "I just wanted you to know I've caught up completely on all my assignments, and I'm making sure I keep on top of all my homework. I'm two chapters ahead in math, and I've read the entire novel for English class." (Well, skimmed it.) I rubbed my eyes convincingly, just to show I hadn't skipped any chapters.

"This is good," Ms. Dreeble said, flipping through the papers of my science assignments. "You've been quite thorough, and you've got the chemistry equations all balanced. That's a nice touch using the different coloured pens. However . . ."

As Ms. Dreeble hesitated, I sucked in my breath. "Howevers" were always a bad sign.

"Cat, on this exchange trip there will be planes to catch, and trains and buses; everyone will have to be prompt. Also, students will have to keep track of luggage and passports and their own money." Ms. Dreeble pronounced the next words much louder and slower. "They will have to listen very carefully and do exactly as they are told. In other words . . ."

I still hadn't breathed. Ms. Dreeble stared at me over her glasses. I looked over her head at the dog-eared periodic table on the wall. And waited.

". . . students will have to be reliable," Ms. Dreeble finished.

Reliability was not what Ms. Dreeble considered one of my strengths. But I wanted to shout, *I am reliable! I saved this town from three terrible disasters*. But the adult world didn't know about fairy trouble—even when it stared them in the face. Everyone in this town only saw the fairy incidents as distant, hazy dreams. Instead, I said with all my heart, "I want to be reliable."

Then Ms. Dreeble said something that surprised me. She said, "I believe you, Cat." She held the reference letter in her hand, the one I desperately wanted her to sign. "Give me a day to think about this."

"It's supposed to be in Ms. Sevren's office by tomorrow," I reminded her. I didn't think it would be easy getting my teachers to sign the letters; still, I'd counted on convincing them. This was so not part of the game plan.

"I'll tell Ms. Sevren I won't have the letters ready until the end of the day," said Ms. Dreeble. "Not to worry."

Easy for her to say.

I'd gone to Ms. Dreeble first because I thought it would be easier to convince her than my history teacher. After all, I liked science and Ms. Dreeble had said my work was good. But she still hadn't signed. Clearly, I'd need a different angle with Mr. Morrows.

When I got to his class I said, "Did I ever tell you that some of my ancestors were Scandinavian?" Faded and crinkled history posters plastered all over his walls had given me an idea to try and get on his good side.

Mr. Morrows was busy marking test papers, and he didn't even look up when he said, "Oh, do tell."

"Well, these ancestors are from a long ways back—Vikings, maybe." I'd have to ask Mom because that part was a little foggy. "I think Vikings are fascinating."

"It won't help, Cat," said Mr. Morrows.

"What won't help?" I could barely speak as my throat started to squeeze shut.

Finally looking up from his marking, Mr. Morrows said seriously, "It won't help to convince me that I should sign your reference letter. You are not pulling a B in my class."

If you averaged out my other marks, I still meet the criteria, my mind screamed. But it was my experience that arguing with teachers never helped.

I slid my letter on his desk. "Just in case you want to think it over." I also handed in an overdue essay and all the finished questions for the next three chapters.

I trudged down the dingy stairwell that was looking even drearier at the moment. For some reason, it felt like I was carrying even more weight in my backpack, even though I'd handed in all my work. I swung by the gym entrance where everyone was still hanging out.

"Cat, we've organized another car wash. It's tomorrow during the rush hour before dinner," said Zach. Even the thin ray of light from Darkmont's tiny window didn't glow over Zach's golden head like it usually did. It was as if I was wearing sunglasses—everything seemed so dark.

"And the first bake sale is Saturday," said Mitch.

"We've also signed you up for the recycling rally, so you need to bring in any metal junk tomorrow morning," said Clive. "We'll be sorting it right after school. Think you can possibly keep all that straight?"

Clive liked giving me a hard time, but he was smiling. Even though he was growing on me, I didn't have the heart to shoot back a smart reply. I just shrugged my shoulders.

"You did say you'd sign up for anything, right?" asked Amarjeet. "Because I'm not getting any volunteers to walk the kindergarten kids from daycare to the elementary school in the morning, and then back again at noon. No one wants to give up their lunch hour, but the daycare's willing to pay us a hundred and fifty bucks." Then she looked over the instruction sheet. "You do have your babysitting certificate, right?"

"Done, done, and done. And yes, I have my certificate." (Mom had made me get it for when I looked after Sookie.) "So done," I said wearily. Then I walked straight out of the school before any of my friends could see me fighting back tears.

All evening I had to pretend my teachers had signed my letters when Mom asked if I'd handed them in. Technically, I had, but not to the vice-principal. But I knew my mom was assuming the trip was on.

In a way, I thought Mom would be okay if I told her I had changed my mind about the trip. There was no need to mention my teachers were changing it for me. Because after Sookie went to bed, I saw her pull out her budget book and spend a lot of time on her computer checking our finances.

That night, I had a nightmare that I was running, and I was sure someone was chasing me. I was glad I'd set my alarm early when I woke up from the creepy dream. Groggily, I rushed out of the house so I could collect and deliver scrap metal to the school. After that, I picked up a bunch of little kids from their daycare and walked them to school.

"Hey, Cat, what are you doing here?" asked Sookie when Amarjeet and I dropped off eight kids at her elementary school. I was exhausted. It had been like chasing a gym full of rolling soccer balls going in every direction.

"Hey," I said right back to my sister. "Why aren't you wearing your new glasses?"

Sookie stuck out her tongue at me and said, "'Cause I see better without them. And there's important stuff I'm watching." Then the bell rang, and she ran off with her friend Skeeter, disappearing into the school with a mob of shrieking kids.

"We better hurry," said Amarjeet. "I got Ms. Sevren to give us permission to be late for first class, but she only gave us fifteen extra minutes." Amarjeet and I jogged the rest of the way back.

At lunch I delivered the kids back to their daycare.

After school I spent over an hour being bossed around by Clive about how to properly prepare all the metal for recycling. "You're right," I couldn't help tell him sarcastically. "There's only one way to remove the labels from cans, otherwise it's the end of the world."

Clive stormed off to boss more willing helpers. Later I joined Zach, Emily, Amanda, and Mitch at the local gas station for the car wash. It started out good for business because our town was small, and all our parents made sure they'd stop by the car wash on their way home from work.

Also, a lot of teachers came. But then the guys got silly and started having soap fights and squirting water around.

"Cut it out," shouted Mia, her face turning as red as her hair. "If we're not serious, we won't get any returning customers."

Mitch squirted Mia in the face with a hose. Mia grabbed a soapy bucket and raced after him to exact her revenge. It wasn't that I didn't want to join in on the water fight; I just didn't have the heart for it. So I found myself, strangely enough, working with Clive, who had signed up for almost as many fundraising events as I had. We kept scrubbing, then hosing down cars, while the others goofed around.

"Good job, you two," said a voice from behind. I turned around.

Ms. Dreeble nodded approvingly at us, while Mr. Morrows had rounded up the others and was now giving them the "Just how badly do you want to go to Sweden?" lecture.

"There's no profit margin in monkey business," Mr. Morrows said. Apparently he thought they didn't want the trip enough.

"We reviewed the sign-up sheets," said Ms. Dreeble. "You've volunteered for every fundraiser. You really want this trip, don't you, Cat?"

I only nodded. While my heart felt it would burst if I didn't go, would it do any good to say so? I didn't have Sookie's skill for dazzling people with words. Instead I just kept my head down, so Ms. Dreeble wouldn't see my stinging eyes.

"I know you are busy, but perhaps you have time to see me before school tomorrow?" asked Ms. Dreeble.

A tiny bubble of hope worked its way into my heart.

CHAPTER 4

AT ALL COSTS

Darkmont High never looked inviting at the best of times. But it took all my courage to walk through its darkened doors in the early morning light. Even the promise of a sky blue afternoon didn't help. While it might almost be spring, somebody forgot to tell the north wind. A chill set my teeth chattering.

I stood outside Ms. Dreeble's classroom. The halls were quiet except for the occasional echo of a teacher's footsteps down the yellowed linoleum hallway. Grey walls pressed in on me. Would my teachers sign my consent forms or not? Finally, I decided it was just better to know and deal with it. I stepped inside the science classroom.

This time I managed not to knock over any stools. Ms. Dreeble sat at her desk, her blond hair tied back, her glasses perched on her nose, and her lab coat already on. She was waiting for me.

"Good morning, Cat. So, I am sure you want to get to the point of this meeting," said Ms. Dreeble. "Well, Mr. Morrows and I have been talking."

So not a good thing.

Ms. Dreeble stared me in the eye. "You know, Cat, I think you need to learn how to be more accountable."

That was teacher-talk for saying I wasn't going on a student exchange anytime soon.

"But it's not just you," she said. "There are many seniors who are not becoming as responsible as they should. Students are handing in assignments late, showing up unprepared for tests, getting distracted when they are supposed to be studying."

It sure sounded like she was only talking about me.

"Sometimes," said Ms. Dreeble, "the way to become more mature is to be given greater responsibilities."

I wasn't sure what she meant, but I nodded furiously and muttered, "Definitely."

"Mr. Morrows is willing to average out your history grade, and we have decided to sign all the reference letters." Ms. Dreeble's grim face made me do a double take. And then I realized what she'd said.

Don't laugh, don't cheer, and don't look too happy. So I kept sombre as I shouted in my mind, *I. Get. To. Go.* But I could feel the corners of my mouth twitch upward.

Ms. Dreeble tapped her pen on her desk. "In exchange we are asking students to sign a contract of responsibility, acknowledging that this trip is a privilege and an opportunity to learn."

As if I was a bobblehead, I kept on nodding.

"Before you sign this contract, I want you to know we're going to have high expectations for every student's behaviour—academically and socially. This will be a very intensive program," Ms. Dreeble warned.

What was that? But still I kept agreeing as I scribbled my signature on the contract before she could change her mind. Then I backed out the door and rushed to pick up the daycare kids. I ran all the way and got there just before Amarjeet.

"What are you so happy about?" she asked miserably as two of the little boys ran away from the group for the third time.

We were in serious danger of not making it back to Darkmont in Ms. Sevren's fifteen-minute window. Getting anxious, Amarjeet said for the third time, "I told you two to stay in line and hold hands."

They didn't seem to care, so I chased after them and said, "Bet you can't hold hands all the way to school. Bet you'll forget and let go."

"I won't forget," said a freckled-face boy.

"Yes, you will," said his dark-haired friend. "I'm going to win."

I grinned and wrangled them back as Amarjeet eyed me suspiciously. My heart soared as if I'd just scored a hat trick in the World Cup, but what could I say? She didn't know how I almost wasn't allowed to go on the exchange. So instead I said, "We're going to Sweden . . . for three weeks . . . on our own!"

"You're right. Even this is worth it." Then Amarjeet ran after two little girls who scampered from the line, wanting to get them in on the bet.

I'll admit it wasn't easy keeping up with all the fundraising projects and homework. Fortunately, I didn't mind the work cutting into my sleep time: that nightmare I kept having was unsettling. It was better to keep busy until I was tired to the bone. Then I'd collapse each night into a deep, dark sleep and not even worry about the nightmare. That is, until I remembered the haunting dream in the morning.

For the next weeks, all my friends and I worked endlessly with car washes, bake sales, and every other possible way to earn money for the trip. Each day in the gym, we marked a thermometer graph that showed how much money we'd raised. As the red line on the graph climbed, the individual cost of our trip went down.

Somehow we had to get the red line to go a lot higher if I was going to have a chance at affording the trip. After school the day before the raffle draw, I stood in the gym staring at the thermometer on the wall. While we'd collected a lot of money, the trip was still expensive when you divided the total among each student. Mom had been pulling out her budget book almost every night this week, and each day when I came home from school she'd ask how much the trip was costing.

I knew this wasn't good.

"Hey, Cat, why don't we try to sell the last bunch of raffle tickets?" suggested Jasper as he joined me in the gym. "This is our last chance before the draw, so we might as well make the best of it."

"Haven't we already hit up every person in town?" I myself had unloaded quite a few tickets at Mr. Keating's Emporium.

"I walked past the Greystones' house this morning," said Jasper. "The curtains were open, and I think they're back from Arizona."

Lucinda Greystone had become ill in February. It had alarmed me that she'd become so frail. Then her sister, Alice, decided a sunny vacation to someplace warm would be for the best until winter was over. "They'll definitely buy tickets," I said enthusiastically. Besides, I wanted to drop by and say hello.

We raced to see the Greystones, who lived in an old-fashioned house with a wraparound porch. Jasper had been right. The porch was swept, and a pot of dirt sat on their top step ready for the bag of tulip bulbs sitting next to it. They were back. We opened their gate to the squeal of a rusty hinge.

"I should fix that hinge for them," said Jasper, swinging the gate back and forth.

Jasper was considerate of others and enjoyed helping out the Greystone sisters. I also knew that he suggested we sell these extra tickets because Jasper understood the expense of the trip wouldn't be easy for my family.

We raced up the steps and pounded the brass door knocker in the shape of a lion's head.

A tanned Alice Greystone answered the door. "Cat, Jasper, come in and say hello," she greeted us enthusiastically.

It was a relief to see Lucinda, and although she didn't stand up, she smiled warmly, and the sparkle was back in her eyes. "Do fill me in on all the news," she said. "And tell me, how is my little friend Sookie doing?"

I understood this to be a loaded question. What Lucinda really wanted to know was if anything magical and troubling was going on with my sister.

"Sookie's playing with Skeeter mostly and doing normal third grade things," I explained.

"As a matter of fact, the only thing wrong with Sookie these days is that she hates her new glasses," I remembered.

"Oh, it's no fun to get glasses," Alice said ruefully. "I remember hating them back in grade school. But it was the only way I could see the chalkboard."

"Funny," I said, "Sookie has the opposite reaction. She gets mad because she says they make everything even harder to see. And she says there are important things she's watching." I laughed, but then I realized no one else in the room was sharing my amusement.

"What?" I asked, confused. And then it hit me—my sister had a tendency for hearing things that nobody else heard. And of seeing things that nobody else saw. "Oh," I said quietly.

"Do you think magic is at work on her again?" Jasper said in alarm.

"Is she doing anything peculiar?" asked Lucinda.

That question was very hard to pin down with Sookie. She was all about the peculiar, but I said, "She's been acting more like her third grade friends than ever. That's a good sign, right?"

Alice nodded and said, "That sounds nice and normal. Don't you worry, Cat. Go on your trip and have a wonderful time. Lucinda and I will keep a close watch on your little sister . . . if there's even anything to watch out for."

Lucinda agreed and then the Greystones bought ten raffle tickets each.

Jasper and I walked home together, and he reassured me, "Sookie will be fine. They will do a better job than us of keeping track of her."

He had that right. My sister rebelled at anything I tried to tell her; she didn't like being bossed around. But she adored Lucinda, and I knew she'd listen to her.

Jasper and I walked back to the school and turned in the tickets and cash. We quickly calculated how much the trip would cost each student, and it was still way more than what I knew Mom could afford. But the draw was closed, and the fundraising was almost over.

And I was running out of time.

CHAPTER 5

AN EERIE PREDICTION

We were hanging out at the soccer field, just kicking around a ball for old times' sake. The air was crisp and had that really fresh scent of spring, like lilacs were on their way.

It had been weeks since the intramural co-ed tournament. We'd come in second, which was only a little disappointing. It had been a close game and hard fought. More importantly, we'd come together as a team. I liked it that way, all of us as a group, so my heart dived at Mia's final fundraising idea.

"We could have another dance," suggested Mia, "and sell tickets."

My foot froze mid-kick. The soccer ball dribbled past me. "Don't even go there," I winced. That event had started out stressful enough with all of us obsessed with who would go to the dance with whom. And then the actual dance had almost ended in death and destruction.

"I hardly remember the Valentine's dance," said Zach. "But I recall it wasn't fun, and I was sick for three days afterwards."

"Yeah," said Rabinder. "I caught that flu that was going around. My parents said I hadn't been myself even before the stupid dance."

"I couldn't keep anything down but liquids for two days," complained Mitch.

"I don't remember having any fun either. That's weird." Amarjeet looked puzzled, and then a shadow crossed her face. She shook her head as if to shake out an unpleasant thought.

The less they remembered the better. Jasper and I exchanged meaningful glances. That had been a horrific night. We both needed to leave Grim Hill behind—even if it was only for a few weeks.

"There's no time for a dance," Clive scowled at Mia as if that was the dumbest thing he'd ever heard. "Our families have to pay for the final cost of the trip by Friday. That means tomorrow is the cutoff for fundraising."

Clive had such a dismissive way of saying things, as if Mia was crazy for even suggesting it. While she sort of was, there was no need to drive it home. Mia flushed and didn't come up with any more suggestions. I didn't think Clive was intentionally cruel all the time, he was just so arrogant. And then it struck me: Clive was desperate to raise as much money as possible, *kind of like me.*

"So what genius idea do you have?" I asked.

For a minute Clive was silent, and I watched his eyes search the soccer field as if he'd find an answer there. Then his eyes lit up when he noticed the trash can. "One massive bottle drive, right here, right now. We divide up into teams and scour the town."

Amarjeet said, "How about the team with the least bottles buys drinks at the Bubble Tea Palace for everyone else?"

Clive scowled again, so before he said something cutting, I broke in. "Maybe we should hold on to our spending money for the trip." But Clive's idea wasn't half bad, and a little competition would keep it interesting.

"The losing team has to sort the bottles and take them to recycling," Clive announced. I passed my hand over his head.

"What?" he said irritably.

"I'm just checking if you have a crown. Somehow you think you've been declared king." But I smiled when I said it. At least he didn't storm off when everyone else laughed. "Girls against guys?" I suggested. But nobody took me up on that idea; instead we played odds and evens.

We divided into two teams. I was with Clive, Jasper, and Amarjeet. Mia, Mitch, Zach, and Amanda were on the other team. We took off.

The first stop was Clive's place, where we picked up garbage bags. Sookie and Skeeter were playing pirates in the backyard. Sookie wore her eye patch and a paper pirate's hat. Her hamster, Buddy, was perched on her shoulder instead of a parrot.

"Hey," I called to Sookie. "What did Mom say about taking Buddy outside? He could run away and get lost."

"No, he couldn't," Sookie said. "I'm not putting him on the ground, so don't boss me around." Then she turned to Skeeter. "Tie up the landlubbers."

"Aye, aye, Captain." Skeeter lurched toward us, brandishing a wooden sword. Jasper laughed, but my experience with Skeeter was to take a step back. *That kid could get carried away,* I thought, just as he knocked over a huge clay pot and scattered dirt all over the patio.

Clive leaned over and grabbed Skeeter's sword. "Better clean that pot up before Gran sees it." Skeeter gulped and went to get a broom.

"See, Cat. You've got to be firm and show your sister who's boss," Clive said arrogantly.

"It's not that easy," complained Amarjeet, whose own kid brother, Raj, was not above blackmail.

When Skeeter came back out and began sweeping, Clive said, "And tell Sookie you should be the captain."

"That's stupid," said Skeeter. "She's got the hat and the eye patch."

"Boss, huh?" I couldn't resist mocking him. We grabbed our bags and began the bottle search. Before we got out of range, Sookie shouted, "Cat, watch out for the water!"

What did she mean by that? Even though Sookie sounded strangely alarmed, I didn't have time to think about it; the sun was going down and we had a lot of ground to cover. I took off with my friends.

We hunted for bottles until my hands and jacket were sticky and my legs and back ached.

"Let's go down to the river for one last sweep," suggested Jasper. There was no way the other team could have collected as many bottles as us, but I went along, and even though she groaned, so did Amarjeet.

The river in our town was swift and deep. But the banks were a gold mine of littered bottles. Pretty soon five of our bags were full, and the last three were close. As we started to leave, I looked over at a deep ditch that cut into the river. "Jackpot," I said.

Beside the charred remains of a campfire were a few dozen bottles. We easily leaped over the wide ditch and collected the bottles. But when we went to jump back, my bag dragged me down at the last second.

"Cat, watch out!" Jasper shouted.

It was too late. I began slipping down the bank into the treacherous current below. I dug in my feet, but sand gave way and I couldn't find my footing. All I could think was that Mom would be so mad at me if I drowned.

Amarjeet grabbed the hood of my jacket and stopped me from sliding. "Let go of the stupid bag, Cat."

I hadn't thought of that. But before I let go, Jasper and Clive grabbed my arms and hauled me up the bank. With a wrenched ankle and a nasty cut on my arm from a rock, I lay down in the sand for a second and listened to the water rush past. How did Sookie know I should watch out for the water? I shivered.

"If it's any consolation," Clive said, I hoped half jokingly, "I think we won the competition." Jasper glared at him.

Sticky and exhausted, I made it back home. I was shaken but not because of the mishap by the ditch or because of Sookie's eerie prediction. We'd calculated our money and it was firm. Mom would have to come up with a pretty big cheque.

Maybe our budget could handle that. But when I got home, Mom was down in the basement mopping up a leak from our hot water tank. I grabbed the string mop and helped soak up the water. It wasn't the best time, but there was no choice. I told her the news.

"I see," said Mom, putting the mops in a bucket. That was all she said. What did that mean? Then she looked me over and said, "You look like you need a good soak in the tub before bed. Better go up quick; the hot water is almost gone."

The warm, soapy suds did relax me, even though I could only fill the tub a quarter full. When I went to bed, relaxed or not, I still had that creepy dream, only this time it was in technicolour.

I am running through the dark, and wherever I am, it's cold. Above me the wind rushes, and its impatient roar makes me want to run faster. Underneath me the ground springs back, but sometimes it's slippery. Keep going, *I think.* Hurry, Cat. *I can't see, but wet tree branches slap against me and their needles prickle. I begin to shiver as icy flakes fall.*

Jump, turn, dodge. I twist my way through the maze, but my legs ache. The wind blasts and soon I'm shrouded with snow. I think I am in a forest—the smell of pine, the sweeping wet branches, needles that crunch under my sneakers. But I'm in the kind of forest where Hansel and Gretel got lost, because in the background I hear a cruel cackle that freezes me from the inside more quickly than any amount of snow. This is the end of me, *I think.*

But I'm wrong.

Wherever I am next, the ground is even less trustworthy as it bucks and dips and sways. I'm holding on so tight my hands feel like claws. Around me the rushing sound changes to a furious slap, slap, moving faster until a crash . . . and I tumble forward.

Splash! Then I am sinking in water colder than anything I've imagined, as if I'd crawled inside a block of ice. I kick my legs and thrash my arms as bubbles of air escape my lungs. On my last kick I feel a tug. Something has grabbed me from below.

Can I scream underwater?

Ring . . . Ring . . . Ring . . . Seconds ticked by. Ring? Then I awoke to the sound of my alarm clock.

When I dragged myself downstairs, Mom was waiting in the kitchen.

"Cat," she called me in, "we need to talk."

I sat down with her at the table. The smell of cinnamon wafted from the oven. Mom was making my favourite: apple muffins. And it wasn't even the weekend. The table had already been set. The red clock above the stove ticked away. A blue curtain fluttered in a window draft.

"What is it, Mom?" I asked.

Mom ran her hands through her blond, wavy hair. She stared at the open finance books on the table.

Then she turned to me and asked, "Just how much are you willing to sacrifice for this trip?"

CHAPTER 6

A DREADFUL DEAL

I would have given anything to go on the student exchange to Sweden. Anything. But this was asking too much. I stared numbly at my black sneakers, then I uttered a horrified, "Nooo."

"Sweetie, I'm sorry but this is the only way." Mom frowned at my reaction. "And with your Aunt Hildegaard's help, there could even be spare cash for a new outfit or two for you and your sister."

"No," I repeated, this time more firmly.

Sookie came into the kitchen, pulling a plaid suitcase behind her. "Should I pack this one, Mom? What's wrong, Cat?"

"Nothing's wrong," Mom said smoothly. "Cat is only worried I feel left out of all the excitement, which I don't," she reassured.

Sookie glanced at me suspiciously, as if she hadn't bought Mom's story, at least, not completely.

"That suitcase will do fine," Mom told her. "Now why don't you take it upstairs and keep it in your room? That way you can start packing."

Sookie shot one more wary look my way and then agreed, thumping the suitcase on every step.

"Why?" I choked. "I don't understand."

"I called your Aunt Hildegaard," explained Mom, "to see if you could stay with her during the trip. That way we'd only have to cover the airfare. But then she generously offered to pay for the trip, as long as she could see *both* of you. She figures it may be her only opportunity to ever meet her grandnieces."

Then I wanted to cover up my ears so I wouldn't hear the rest of what Mom was saying.

"I talked to your teachers and the school principal," said Mom. "They agreed that Sookie could come along on the exchange and stay with the group in Stockholm until you meet up with your aunt, as long as you mind her for those few days."

"There must be some other way," I complained. "I've never even heard of this aunt."

"Sure you have, sweetie," said Mom in that kind of fake cheerfulness she used when she needed us to see the upside. "She's your great-aunt, actually. You've never met her, but I've told you the story of when I stayed with her on her farm. That was a special summer for me."

I vaguely remembered but kept shaking my head. There was no way I'd want to go on the trip and not stay with everyone else. Not to mention the biggest reason—

"Mom, will I need my bathing suit?" Sookie called downstairs.

"No!" I shouted. *Because you won't be going*, I said to myself.

Mom rubbed her forehead, which was creased with worry. I didn't like upsetting her, but this wouldn't work. All my friends would be sharing rooms in a hotel and having fun and hanging out. Meanwhile, I'd be stuck with my kid sister and with some relative I'd hardly even heard of. Sometimes a person has got to dig in her heels.

"There is no other way," Mom said firmly. "The hot water tank needs to be replaced. My salary goes down by half in the summer, since the school only needs a part-time secretary. Sookie's glasses cost . . . Well, these things aren't for you to worry about, Cat, but I can't just ignore them. The bottom line is that I would love for you to go on this trip. With a more positive attitude, you'll have an amazing time."

Then Mom sighed and closed the budget book with a thump. "That's my offer. Take it or leave it."

Sometimes there's no point in a person digging in her heels. "I'll take it," I said quietly.

That night when the nightmare came, I couldn't sort out if I was fleeing in terror with my kid sister or if she was the one chasing me.

"You set a bad precedent," complained Clive.

He'd met me at my locker just before class. "What do you mean?" I asked briskly. I didn't have the patience for

Clive's attitude this morning, not after what Mom had sprung on me. I pulled out my chemistry book.

"Skeeter's been at my grandmother all morning. What is your mom thinking, sending your kid sister with you? If my gran decides he gets to go—"

"First," I said as annoyance crept into my voice, "my mom's got no choice. Our aunt wants to see both of us." I didn't see the point in mentioning the family finances; that was none of Clive's business. "So unless you have Swedish relatives that are willing to let Skeeter stay with them, my guess is you're safe. Plus, we both know no teachers would take him on." This time I tried a smile, but my mouth didn't move much.

Instead of being snotty, Clive said, "I hadn't thought of that." What was that look in his eye? Sympathy? I'd rather see him sneer.

Later at lunch, Mia said, "Oh, Cat, I had so many plans. The three of us would have been roommates and stayed up late and well . . ."

"Now we'll have to room with someone else. What if she's a snob or wants us to stay quiet?" Amarjeet complained.

My blood was ready to boil, and I wanted to explode at someone. At my friends for thinking this was my idea, or at my mom for setting this up, or at Sookie for being so ecstatic about tagging along.

Emily walked by, dragging her feet. She went over to the cool kids' table, where we were almost eligible to sit if only there was enough room on the benches. Emily thumped her tray down on the table, and chocolate milk sloshed onto her sandwich.

"Wow," I said, happy to redirect the conversation and cool my temper. "What's her problem?"

"Haven't you heard?" said Mia. "Her parents had already booked a family vacation over spring break. They're making her go, and she can't come to Sweden."

I let out a low whistle. And I thought I had problems. At least I was going. Then it hit me: just because something wasn't perfect didn't mean I had to feel miserable. I'd make this trip work.

I'd spend every moment I could with my friends, and as for Sookie, well, she'd just have to find a way to keep herself amused on Aunt Hildegaard's farm.

So I made a deal with myself, a deal to have fun no matter what. Then the clouds in the sky rolled away and the sun lit the courtyard outside the cafeteria. Sun shone through the glass doors, lighting up the drab cafeteria and shooting rays onto our table.

But while my friends basked in the warmth, my body gave a slight shiver. I couldn't help remembering that good things around here were never what they seemed.

CHAPTER 7

ALWAYS BE PREPARED

"You're not going to need that bathing suit," I told my sister for the tenth time.

"But Mom said Aunt Hildegaard has a farm by a lake." Sookie tried stuffing the suit into her bulging plaid suitcase.

"It's still too cold for swimming here, and Sweden's by the Arctic Circle. That lake's probably frozen over," I explained. "Ms. Dreeble told us to pack warm sweaters and our winter jackets." I checked out my sister's suitcase. There wasn't room left for a sock let alone a coat. "Is that Buddy's cage?" I asked, suddenly suspicious of the shape of one of the dresses jammed inside her luggage.

"No hamsters are allowed on the plane," Mom said, coming into Sookie's room. She pulled out Buddy's cage and, holding it in one hand, went to Sookie's desk and started shoving papers and colouring pens and books and clothes to one side. Then she placed Buddy's cage on the desk. "I promise to take good care of him. There, now you'll have room for a coat and swimsuit."

Sookie stuck out her tongue at me when Mom's back was turned, and then she went over to her desk and started scribbling. "Okay, but I'm going to give you a list of instructions. Buddy likes to sit in the sun in the morning, and this is the music he likes to listen to when he spins on his wheel." Sookie picked up a different coloured pen and kept writing.

"He likes caraway seeds for breakfast," Sookie said, "and greens for lunch. And he likes sunflower seeds for dinner." She kept on writing. Mom would have a full-time job taking care of that hamster. I backed out of the room and left them to it.

I figured I could carry my coat on the plane, and that would leave more room in my suitcase. Except, I didn't need a whole lot of room. I stared at my almost empty closet.

"Maybe you'd like to pack these?" Mom brought bags into my room and pulled out a new jacket, a sweater, a cool pair of jeans, and a huge shoebox. "Oh, Mom, I always wanted a pair of these."

They were those suede boots with soft lining that felt like cozy slippers when you put them on. They were grey and high enough for me to tuck in my jeans. "I love them."

"And you'll need spending money," said Mom. "I'll let you be in charge of Sookie's money as well." Mom handed me krona, the Swedish currency. "The rest are in traveller's cheque. You should give those to Aunt Hildegaard for safekeeping."

"What's Sweden like?" I asked.

Mom's face grew warm as she basked in the happy memory. "The summer I spent in Sweden was wonderful. Warm—but not too hot—and so peaceful. I remember the lake and sky being such a beautiful blue. And the northern lights," Mom said excitedly. "I saw them three times that summer, and I've never seen them since."

Then Mom grew thoughtful. "Your aunt Hildegaard must be getting on," she said. "I've just realized—she was quite old when I was a girl. Cat, you've got to promise me that you two won't be any trouble. You've got to keep a close eye on your sister so she doesn't wear your aunt out."

Just then there was a shriek in Sookie's room. Then she came running in and started an excited babble. "I just looked up Sweden in a book my teacher gave me. Did you know Santa's reindeers live there? Oh, Cat, we've just got to see them as soon as we get there. Do you think any live on Aunt Hildegaard's farm? This is stupendous!

"And in Stockholm there's a butterfly house you can visit any time of year. We've got to go to that." Sookie started dancing in a circle. "And there's a fantasy park just for kids with a statue of Pippi Longstocking," she almost squealed in delight. "We've got to go there, too."

Sookie pulled her patch up over her head. "There are no pirates, but there's something even more astounding: Vikings!"

As my kid sister kept babbling, the first few days I'd planned in Sweden were going up in flames. Our aunt wouldn't be meeting us until we went to the town close to her farm. I was stuck with Sookie until then, and my friends and I talked about going sightseeing in Stockholm. There was no way I wanted to take Sookie to do that dumb kid stuff. We all wanted to go to Gröna Lund, the big amusement park Zach had heard about.

Maybe we could get Sookie to go to bed early and leave her at the hotel. Then Sookie said, "And the sun stays high in the sky starting in spring. It doesn't set until about ten at night there, so we can stay awake really late."

"Well, it's plenty dark here, missy, and it's time for you to go to bed. We have to get up very early to drive to the airport." Mom ushered Sookie out of my room. "I think we'd better have one more look at what you've packed before you go to sleep."

After they left, I sat down on the hard window seat and stared out past our backyard fence. Grim Hill loomed in the distance, and I'd never seen it appear so undisturbed. Not a single weird light flashed back from the hill, or any strange clouds. Instead, a crescent moon hung low in the clear night sky, and the trees on the hill were hidden in shadow.

I fiddled with the silky white feather I always kept on a thin silver chain clasped to my waist. I unhooked it and was about to dump it in my drawer, and then hesitated. Even though I wasn't going to need glamour protection in

Sweden, I'd promised Lucinda I'd always keep it with me. I slipped the chain and feather into a pocket in my suitcase.

When it comes to fairies, you always want to be prepared.

CHAPTER 8

JOURNEY INTO THE UNKNOWN

The airport bustled with activity. For the third time, Mr. Morrows and Ms. Dreeble tried hustling us into an organized group, which wasn't going to happen anytime soon. A bunch of parents and even the Greystone sisters had come to see us off. There was too much hugging, and too many "I'll miss yous," and too much frantic searching for passports.

And too much Sookie! When our teachers were assigning seats for the plane, Ms. Dreeble joined me in the crowd.

"We're trying to find a third person to sit with you and your sister," Ms. Dreeble said. "But if you can find two other friends to sit with you, we'll put you in a centre aisle."

I looked over my shoulder at my kid sister. She stood there with her plaid suitcase, wearing her floppy wool hat. Why would any of my friends want to sit with her when even I didn't? Then a feeling of guilt crept up on me. It wasn't that I didn't *want* to sit with her, I just wanted to hang out with my friends more. Amarjeet and Mia had secured a row of three seats right in front of Mitch, Rabinder, and Zach. Mia and Amarjeet glanced at me anxiously, and then at the guys. And waited.

"I'll sit with you, Cat," Jasper said, and he waved to Sookie. Excited, she waved back.

"You're a good friend," I shook my head. "You do realize you're in for twelve hours of Monopoly." But Jasper just shrugged his shoulders. I still needed one more person.

"I'll sit with you," Clive said. I turned in surprise. He just smirked and said, "Uh, I'm a big fan of Monopoly. I, uh, love the game."

Ms. Dreeble thanked us and rejoined Mr. Morrows at the counter where they finalized the seating.

Amarjeet and Mia sent sympathetic looks my way before they got Amanda on board for the third seat. The next twelve hours were going to be filled with Monopoly and listening to Clive tell us how we should play the game. This was going to be a *really* long flight.

We joined Mom and the Greystones for one last goodbye. As Mom hugged Sookie for about the thirtieth time, Lucinda took me aside.

"Cat," she said, uncertainty creeping into her voice, "I'm not quite sure how to tell you this, so I'll just say it. Be careful."

I liked that Lucinda spoke to me like an equal. Perhaps this was because she'd had to age seventy years in mere hours after she was released from the fairy world. But still my throat tightened. "Is it Sookie?" I wished more than ever that my little sister was staying behind under their watchful care.

Lucinda shook her head and in a hesitant voice said, "It's nothing clear, but I've been having a recurring dream that could be a warning."

My heart thumped in my chest.

"This dream is about a fairy tale that used to frighten me as a child: the story of Hansel and Gretel. In my dream they are far off in the distance. I can't quite make out their faces, but there's a girl that looks a bit like you, Cat, and a boy holding her hand in a malevolent forest. And I hear the witch cackling behind the trees." Lucinda shook her head. "I used to wake up scared before I remembered that it was just a dream. Now, it's a feeling of mild dread I can't shake."

Hansel and Gretel? That wasn't so bad. Except now that Lucinda mentioned it, my own dream was about a dark and dangerous-looking forest. I said warily, "Do you think that dream has something to do with the trip?"

I took a breath and waited.

Lucinda fastened me with a stare. "There's no way to say for sure. I just want you to stay alert. Did you bring your feather?"

I nodded. I wasn't wearing it, but it was still in my suitcase.

At that, relief washed over Lucinda's face. "Good."

Then Mom came over and hugged me *again*. "Have a wonderful trip," she said.

"Thanks." I hugged her back as I watched Lucinda and Alice Greystone. Lucinda was smiling again, and Alice waved goodbye. We were getting away from Grim Hill, so I was sure I wouldn't even need the feather. But if it made Lucinda feel better, I'd keep it close by.

As we gathered to go through the security gate, Sookie let out a squeal of alarm. The security guard did a surprised double take. Ms. Dreeble and Mr. Morrows rushed toward us, and my friends all looked at us at once. My face burned.

"Shh," I hissed. "What's wrong?" On the other side of the gate, Mom's expression flashed with such alarm she may as well have shouted, "Let's pull the plug on the whole trip."

Sookie said, "Cat, I just saw something scary."

The security guard became alert and flashed his eyes across the concourse.

"What? Where?" I said in confusion.

"In the future," Sookie said, and the security guard's wary expression changed to annoyance as he shook his head.

"Maybe your new glasses are playing tricks on you." I tried getting her to change the subject.

"No." Now Sookie sounded irritated. "I'm telling you I can see stuff that's going to happen."

"Shh, you can't see the future," I said as blood raced through my veins. Mr. Morrows and Ms. Dreeble arrived.

I must have said that kind of loud because Zach shouted, "Cool, can I try those glasses on?"

Then my friends laughed, and for a second I thought Sookie was going to get mad, but she smiled and said, "Please keep them. They just get in the way." She handed the glasses off to Zach, and we watched him model them for everyone. Personally, I thought Amanda laughed a bit too loudly. At least Sookie settled down, and our teachers drifted to the back of the line. Mom looked relieved and waved to us as we finally passed through the gate.

But as we headed toward the departure lounge, I whispered to Sookie, just to be sure, "Did you mean you think you're in danger?"

Sookie shook her head and said with a sniff, "No, Cat. *You're* the one who's in danger."

CHAPTER 9

LAND OF THE MIDNIGHT SUN

After we landed near Stockholm, we stumbled exhausted from the plane and onto an airport transport bus that would take us into the city centre to our hotel. Sitting on the bus, I was pretty amazed. Stockholm was like nothing I'd ever seen.

As we travelled over bridge after bridge, Ms. Dreeble explained, "Stockholm is an archipelago of thousands of islands, with the fourteen main islands connected by bridges."

Houses crept down to the water's edge where the ocean and canals met the city; they were old red-brick houses, some made of yellow and orange stone. All the houses had high-pitched roofs. The tiny wood-framed windows puzzled me until I realized that this was a cold climate, and the last thing you'd need were big, drafty windows.

The ground still had a dusting of snow in the middle of April, and along the water's edge were tree-lined pathways and cafés with iron gates and balconies.

Narrow cobblestone streets spread like a labyrinth behind the houses. I squirmed excitedly in my seat as I ached to go out and explore. My sister snoozed beside me on my left, and Jasper snored softly to my right. Someone in the back was snorting annoyingly loud, but when I turned to complain, I realized it was Mr. Morrows. Then I stifled a huge yawn—it had been almost twenty hours since I'd slept.

When the bus pulled up outside our small hotel, I stepped out into the lemony sunlight. Even though it was eight at night in Sweden, there was still daylight. But it was cold, and unlike the chill in our town, this cold had a dampness that seeped into my bones. I hugged my coat closer as a groggy Sookie asked, "Are we there yet?"

"Yep," I said, stifling another yawn and helping her with her suitcase.

Rock music drifted from up the street where there was a stadium. The hotel valet greeted us with, "*God dag*," which I figured meant "hello," then in English he explained about the music. "This is the entertainment district. It can be quite busy late into the night."

"Cool," a bunch of us said.

Ms. Dreeble and Mr. Morrows didn't look as excited.

The air smelled crisp from fresh snow, and there was also a salty tang from the Baltic Sea. Funny, but I got a sort of hollowness in my stomach, as if my brain was just now taking in that I was a long way from home. But that feeling quickly passed as we were each assigned to our rooms for the night.

It was supposed to be three to a room, but a hotel person ordered a small cot to be brought in for Sookie. Amarjeet, Mia, Sookie, and I sleepily trundled up sixty steps to our room. There weren't elevators, and we had to drag our luggage up the steps.

Our room was small with cheery floral wallpaper, and we had to stash our suitcases under the beds. It was hard work convincing Sookie to brush her teeth, and I could tell Mia and Amarjeet were already getting annoyed with her as a roommate. When Sookie and I came back from the bathroom, I overheard Mia whispering, "We won't be able to stay up late and talk about the guys."

"Yeah," complained Amarjeet. "Sookie will either let something slip accidentally . . . or on purpose." Fortunately, Sookie was too sleepy to figure out they were complaining about her. As a matter of fact, no one had to worry about overheard gossip when we turned out the lights. Despite this being the first night without parents, once we slipped under the heavy feather quilts, it didn't matter that the last weak rays of sunlight still shone through our shuttered window. Or that thrums of electric guitars and banging drums reached the fourth floor of our hotel from the streets below.

We all fell instantly asleep.

I'm falling. I tumble head over heels and splash! I'm plunging into icy water. My body submerges deeper and deeper in the aching cold, and I realize I'm descending toward my doom.

I awoke with a start. Sookie had pulled the quilt off my side of the bed, and I'd rolled into a shivering ball. I tugged the quilt back, but I tossed and turned unable to drift back to sleep.

This was definitely a recurring dream. Lucinda had said that recurring dreams could be warnings. But her dream was about Hansel and Gretel. What kind of warning could that be?

Then there was Sookie. What did she mean at the airport about *seeing* danger in my future? My stomach churned. When it's dark and you're the only one awake, it's like the whole world weighs heavily on your shoulders.

With blurry eyes, I checked my watch on the nightstand. I had reset it to Swedish time when the plane had landed. It was four-thirty in the morning—a world record for me, as I wasn't exactly an early riser. Neither was Sookie, and she snored softly while I lay under the quilt, worrying and waiting for everyone else to wake up.

I must have eventually drifted back to sleep because a knock on our door woke me. "Time to get up," came Ms. Dreeble's voice from the corridor. "We're going to have a breakfast meeting in the dining room. Rise and shine and be downstairs in twenty minutes."

Amarjeet groaned and Mia yawned. Sookie remained unconscious. We quickly washed up, and I yanked on the new jacket Mom had bought me. Mia and Amarjeet headed for the dining room as I tried hauling Sookie out of bed. She was unhappy about it, but I wasn't about to be late after promising Ms. Dreeble that I would be more responsible.

As we raced down the endless steps, it occurred to me I wasn't feeling worried anymore. The daylight seemed to put everything into perspective. Dreams are just symbols of whatever is on our minds. I was in Sweden and I knew there were lots of forests and waterways here. Big deal. And given all the bad fairy magic Lucinda had faced, she'd naturally have bad dreams about fairy tales. As for Sookie . . .

But I didn't have time to consider what was going on with my sister because we arrived in the hotel dining room ten minutes late and had missed the opening of the meeting. You could sense the excitement in the air when Sookie and I took a seat at an empty table. Amarjeet and Mia had joined Amanda, leaving only one available seat at their table. Everyone was grouped in fours, and I winced, wondering if my sister would be my only partner for our stay in Stockholm.

Resentment burned in me as Sookie complained, "What kind of breakfast is this? It looks more like a lunch. Where are the frosty oats?"

"When in Rome, do as the Romans do," I replied coolly.

"What's that supposed to mean?" she asked with a frown.

"Forget about what you eat at home, and enjoy the bread and cheese."

"Not for breakfast!" she said stubbornly.

I sighed.

"Cat, did you get the last bit of instructions?" Mr. Morrows asked.

He knew I hadn't, and this was his way of putting me on the spot so everyone else would pay attention. A couple of tables down, Jasper pointed to our tourist passes and to an extremely long checklist of museum sites.

"We're only here for one day, and there's a lot to cover, so no fooling around?" I figured that was an educated guess.

Mr. Morrow's eyes flashed in surprise, and then he quickly nodded, saying, "That's right. We'll explore medieval Stockholm first and then take a ferry to the main museum and tourist sites. For the old part of the city, you are going to meet some of the students from your Swedish sister school, who will be your tour guides. There will be an older student managing each team. I want Darkmont students to show them complete cooperation."

Everyone groaned. He was treating us as if we were primary students. We were too old for buddies.

Hearing our dissatisfaction, Mr. Morrows added, "We can split up on the island at the amusement park, but you will have to check in with Ms. Dreeble and myself every two hours. Understood?"

All of us nodded halfheartedly as we stared at that incredibly long itinerary. How many museums could a person absorb in one full day? After the teachers left the dining room, Zach and Mitch signalled us over to their table. I left my sister, who was still grumbling over a lack of frosty oats.

"Check out our tourist passes," Zach said excitedly. "Besides the museums, they give us free admission to Gröna Lund amusement park," Mitch had spread a map out on their table. "Which happens to be on the same island as the museums we're supposed to see."

"So we work in teams to cover the museum sites," Zach continued. "Then we'll have plenty of time to hit the amusement park."

Even Clive the history nut and Jasper the bookworm seemed impressed. All of us agreed.

Now I just needed to get rid of Sookie.

CHAPTER 10
BEWITCHED

We had already divided ourselves into groups when Mr. Morrows said, “Not a chance. You’re not only socializing with your friends. This is supposed to be an educational activity.” Then he and Ms. Dreeble passed around a hat that was stuffed with cards and told us to choose one.

Mia said, “If we all choose the same colour, then we’ll still be in the same group anyways.”

Amarjeet pulled a blue square out of the hat and examined it. “But they’re also numbered. This one’s a four.”

“Rats,” said Mia. “So do we go for the number or the colour?” Her hand hovered over the hat as she waffled.

“Well, there’s always the totally random method,” I said, closing my eyes and reaching. I scooped out a red square. Turning it over, I saw the number five written on the other side.

“Colour, or number?” Mia muttered frantically as she looked at my red square and Amarjeet’s blue one. Mitch grabbed an orange square.

"Mia, take a card. Now!" Mr. Morrows warned.

With a gulp, Mia grabbed an orange square. The hat travelled down the line of kids, and then Mr. Morrows and Ms. Dreeble divided us into numbers, and then from that group into colours. In a way it was for the best, considering the embarrassment Sookie would cause.

"Is everything okay?" Our tour guide, Anne Britt, had stopped our group and was checking up on Sookie. Again.

Anne Britt was a senior high school student. I'd been expecting someone just a little older than us, as I'd assumed our sister school was a junior high like ours. Her pale, freckled face twitched with a frown she was trying to hold back. I recognized that disappointed expression; she hadn't anticipated being in charge of younger students, or someone as little as Sookie.

With a toss of her reddish-blond hair, Anne Britt said, "We need to move a little faster to catch the Changing of the Guard at the palace."

"My feet hurt and I'm bored," Sookie said. She had stopped walking of her own accord, and it was as if a huge anchor had been tied to my arm. We were in Gamla Stan, the old part of the city, and it was hard enough navigating through winding narrow streets crammed with tourists without dragging her around.

We needed to cross off the Changing of the Guard at the Royal Palace from our list, so I kept pulling Sookie along while we crisscrossed cobblestone pathways. Sookie slowed down as we passed a café where a waiter carried a huge tray piled with pastries. "I'm hungry. I want to see Pippi Longstocking's museum," Sookie mentioned for the fourteenth time.

"You should have eaten breakfast." By now we were trailing far behind my group, and Anne Britt, waiting for us to catch up, was tapping her foot as her green eyes flashed impatiently. A sense of urgency rose inside me. I'd promised my teachers I'd be reliable and hard working on this trip, and responsible. *But how can you be responsible for someone else?* I thought as I glared at Sookie.

"Cat, look at this place," Sookie said with enthusiasm. "Can we go inside, please?"

The peculiar shop had a black cat snoozing in the window. A huge stuffed witch sat in a rocking chair and figurines of elves and trolls crowded the window. We had to hurry; Anne Britt and our group had turned down a street and were out of sight. If we got separated, I'd never find them in this maze. I yanked Sookie's arm and pulled her away from the shop window. By sheer luck we found our group and followed them through the flag-festooned medieval streets, catching the tail end of the guard change at the palace.

"On to the Royal Library," said Anne Britt, stifling a yawn. I could tell she really wanted to be with students her own age.

Then a kid named Joey brought out a map of the library and showed us a route he'd scribbled. "If we stick to this route, we'll be out of the library in twenty minutes, as long as we run." Anne Britt frowned, but she shrugged her shoulders. Everyone took off, and when I turned to grab Sookie's hand—

She was gone.

It wasn't that I didn't know where Sookie had gone, it was that I didn't know how to get there. I'd followed the group without paying attention to landmarks. How was I supposed to find my sister in this maze of streets? And when I found the shop, there was no guarantee that I'd find her inside. I took off in a run.

And I kept running for the next twenty minutes. A stitch clawed at my side. Ignoring it, I forced myself to pay close attention to bridges crossed, paths turned right or left, just so I wouldn't run in circles. But I soon found myself hopelessly trapped inside the twists and turns of the island.

I didn't know what to do, so I pulled out my map again and looked at the street signs. But I hadn't paid attention to the street name that the shop was on. Using the map, I navigated my way back to the palace hoping I'd see something to jog my memory. Relief rushed over me as I saw Jasper's group.

"How's your list going?" asked Jasper. "We're almost done, so we'll be off to the amusement park for sure."

"I've lost Sookie," I said fighting back tears, and I told Jasper what happened.

"Think," Jasper rubbed his head. "What else do you remember about the street the shop was on? Or can you remember something you saw just before that street?"

I closed my eyes. Sookie had been complaining . . . about eating! There was a café. Actually, there had been a lot of cafés on that promenade. I remembered smelling delicious coffee everywhere.

"The shop was near a promenade that had lots of cafés," I said. We took off and as we ran I could hear Jasper's group leader shouting for him to return.

"Helga is going to kill me." Jasper shrugged his shoulders. "Our group leader has a temper." But he didn't seem that worried.

Jasper and I described the promenade to passersby. We'd greet them with "*god dag*" and then launch into English. Fortunately, a lot of people spoke English, and we were soon redirected to the promenade.

A bell rang mournfully as we entered the shop. I didn't know where to look first—strange books written in runes lined a shelf on one side of the shop, and along the other wall the shelf was crowded with little straw broomsticks, crystal balls, and mirrors with strange creatures carved into their wood frames. Tables were crammed with figurines made from felt and clay and porcelain.

Sookie was holding a figurine of red and green felt and asked the shopkeeper, "Is this supposed to be one of Santa's elves?"

I wanted to explode. Here I was panicking through the streets of Stockholm while she was pleasantly passing the time. She was also sipping a cup of milk and munching a cookie at the pay counter.

"Sookie," I began menacingly.

"Ah," said the shopkeeper. She was a tall woman with long grey hair; the colour of her hair matched her eyes exactly. Yet her skin was smooth and she didn't look any older than Ms. Dreeble. "I've been worried about this little one. She said she was part of a school exchange, but I've never heard of such a young person left alone while on a school trip."

"I'm the exchange student. She's just tagging along with us until we get to my aunt's farm," I explained, my face burning.

The woman shook her head in disapproval. "I even called my friend for advice. She's going to drop by." The woman's voice lowered to a whisper. "I also called the police, even though your little sister said she wasn't lost. They're on their way."

I could see it all now: the police, the teachers, my aunt . . . "Let's go," I said to Sookie. Then I turned to the shopkeeper and said, "Thank you."

"My pleasure," said the woman. "Your sister is . . . very interesting."

Sookie kept ignoring me and asked again, "Are these elves?"

The woman took the figurine into her hand and said,

"These are tomtars. They come out at night in the countryside and watch over farms. Did you want to take one home? They're supposed to be good luck."

Instead, Sookie grabbed a creepy figurine. "What about this? Can I buy this as a souvenir?"

"You are the strange one," said the shopkeeper with a smile. "Trolls aren't lucky at all. They are quite evil."

"We should hurry," urged Jasper. But Sookie insisted on making purchases while my blood boiled.

"How did you find your way back here on your own?" I asked under my breath as the woman put the troll in a felt bag. The bell at the door trilled again.

"That's how," Sookie said pointing to the bell. "I heard the bell and followed the sound."

"That's impossible," I said. "This shop is a twenty-minute walk from the palace."

Sookie just shrugged her shoulders and said with a snort, "The shopkeeper believed me."

"Cat, we better go," Jasper said again. If Jasper the perfect student was worried about getting into trouble, I didn't want to imagine what would happen to me.

"Very impressive," said a voice behind us. "So you followed the bell? I'm glad to hear you won't need my services." Thinking the police had arrived, I could feel my heart dive. Instead of the police, a woman who looked like a movie star stood in front of us in a black fur trimmed coat and matching boots. Her vivid blue eyes sparked against her shiny dark hair. We rushed past her as she joined the shopkeeper at the front of the shop. "So your little exchange student has been found."

"I was never lost," corrected Sookie as we dragged her toward the door.

"Thanks again for everything," I said. We rushed out the door with Sookie in tow.

"Are we going to see Pippi Longstocking now?" Sookie asked.

Jasper and I said nothing. Grimly, we rushed through the streets. At least we got away before the police came so my teachers could be left in the dark. That is, if our group guides weren't reporting us missing this minute.

"There's the dome-shaped building at the edge of the entertainment district," said Jasper. "We're close to the hotel."

We rejoined our groups in the lobby. Anne Britt and Helga from Jasper's group seemed relieved to see us. I guess they didn't want to admit we'd gone missing while they were in charge. I shot them a sympathetic look as I rolled my eyes at Sookie.

The main thing was that we got away with it. We'd be able to go to Gröna Lund after all.

Our teachers joined us for lunch in the dining room. After lunch Ms. Dreeble announced, "The headmistress of your sister school, Svartberg Academy, has come into the city to meet you. Please say hello to Ms. Grimmaar."

Sookie waved cheerfully, and the headmistress waved back. The bite of my sandwich stuck in my throat.

It was the woman from the shop.

CHAPTER 11

DARK AMUSEMENT

Sweat beaded inside the collar of my jacket as Ms. Grimmaar made her introductions and announcements. Any second she would walk over and lecture Sookie, Jasper, and me about splitting up from the group. Then Mr. Morrows and Ms. Dreeble would give me their "We're very disappointed in you, Cat" expressions *again*. Even Jasper looked crestfallen. We both pushed the rest of our lunch away, exchanging worried glances.

But neither of my teachers beckoned me, not even when we gathered back into groups and prepared for the second half of the museum excursion. Then Ms. Grimmaar moved toward us. *Here it comes*, I thought. I grabbed Sookie's hand.

Sookie pulled her hand back. "Ouch," she complained.

Anne Britt paled, which wasn't easy with her fair complexion. We were in deep. Ms. Grimmaar loomed over us, and a shadow crept over my heart. Then she smiled.

Winking, she whispered like our co-conspirator, "So, little one, let's see your souvenir."

With a gleeful grin, Sookie yanked out the disgusting troll figurine. Ms. Grimmaar said, “Isn’t he lovely? You’ve chosen a good little helper.”

“I thought the tomtars were good luck dolls.” Sookie looked upon her troll with eyes widened in delight, as if it was a glamorous fashion doll. “But I preferred something more . . . gruesome.”

Ms. Grimmaar patted Sookie’s head and smiled at me. “The part about luck depends on your point of view. There are many ways to interpret Swedish legends.”

“Are we going to see Pippi Longstocking?”

I had to hand it to my sister: she never gave up.

“We’ll see what we can arrange, little one,” said Ms. Grimmaar with another wink at me. “I have a desire to see that museum one more time myself.”

I felt heady with relief. Could I possibly have solved my Sookie problem? With enthusiasm, I joined my group and we all caught the ferry to Djurgarden, an island with more museums and the amusement park. Sookie stuck with Ms. Grimmaar, Mr. Morrows, and Ms. Dreeble the whole time we were on the ferry.

Finally, I could have some fun.

There was only so much my eyes could take in at the Nordic Museum. Even with our group splitting up on different floors so we could share information and check off Mr. Morrows’s endless list, my feet still began to ache.

The outdoor museum had been fun, and the Maritime Museum with the old warship was cool, but I'd had enough of fashion through the ages.

The problem was Mr. Morrows could go on forever; he was a history maniac. We were all beginning to complain, even the tour guides. Finally, Ms. Grimmaar had a short conference with our teachers, and then Mr. Morrows announced, "Ms. Grimmaar has pointed out we'll be doing other museum excursions during the exchange. So we propose that you take the rest of the evening and enjoy the amusement park."

All of Stockholm must have heard us shout. Suddenly, my feet didn't hurt a bit. Best of all, Ms. Dreeble and Ms. Grimmaar promised Sookie they'd take her to the children's fantasyland, and she could get her fill of Pippi Longstocking.

We scuttled in all directions like beetles released from under a rock into the sun. Gröna Lund was perched on the edge of the island, and as dusk deepened, the old-fashioned rides lit up, and the coloured lights flickered in the darkening shadows.

I stuck with Jasper, Rabinder, Clive, and Amarjeet because it was easy to track their dark hair bobbing in a sea of blond heads. Mitch, Amanda, Mia, and Zach must have decided the same thing, and soon we were all roaming the park together.

We dared each other to ride the Power Tower. It seemed like a cool idea, especially when we slowly rose to the top and could scan Stockholm's archipelago. But that only lasted five seconds. Then my heart plummeted along with my stomach as we dropped almost four hundred feet in free fall. I screamed so much my throat was raw and my ears rang. Talk about awesome!

But nobody dared each other to go up again.

Instead we rode bumper cars and Clive kept ramming mine until I was jammed into a corner while everyone else sped around us. I backed my car up and drove it forward with such force that I jarred Clive's car, and it spun away. I got moving again only for the bell to ring and the ride to be over.

Then we all ran and caught a ride on the towering Ferris wheel. Before I could do anything, Clive jumped into my cart. Amarjeet shot me a sympathetic glance when Zach climbed in beside Amanda. As if the fates were against me, the wheel stopped while our cart was near the top, and we swung over the water.

"This is the best time I've ever had." Clive leaned over, tilting our cart forward. *Me too*, I thought in surprise, even though Clive had been shadowing me the whole time. I joined in to see how hard we could swing it back and forth. Then Amanda and Zach's cart directly above us started doing the same, then Mitch and Mia's cart below. The ride manager yelled up in Swedish. We didn't need a translator; we understood he was telling us, "Cut it out!"

"Look at the lights on the water," said Clive. "I'd like to grab a camera or a paint brush and capture it forever." He pointed at the water's edge. The carnival lights danced on the sea's currents, blurring the colours together. I didn't know Clive had an artistic side.

"This place is so great, and I'm having the best time," I said, a little more awkwardly than I'd intended.

"It's always more fun when all you have to care about is yourself."

Again, it was as if Clive knew exactly what I was feeling. Then he pointed at his watch and his smile dimmed. "We've got to meet back with the teachers soon. I can't wait until I'm old enough to stay out as late as I want," he complained.

"That goes without saying," I agreed, not wanting this evening to ever end.

After we left the Ferris wheel, Zach got the idea to ride the carousel, even though it looked like a little kid's ride. But we all agreed and climbed onto horses that lurched forward with the squeal of ancient machinery after the sound of a bell. Suddenly, Zach reached over and swept me onto his horse. Then everyone started goofing around and laughing. But Clive, sitting on the horse beside ours, kept sending me mutinous looks. Then Amanda, who had taken the horse ahead of us, looked behind her shoulder and glared daggers at me.

After the carousel the girls and guys argued over staying at the rides or spending the remaining time at the arcades.

"Let's flip a coin," said Mitch. "Heads or tails?"

We lost. But I wasn't really interested in watching them all show off at the arcade. Who cares how many plastic ducks a person shoots? Instead, Amarjeet and I broke away and wandered the fairground. The sawdust and diesel smells hung in the air, and soon we stumbled upon a small tent displaying a line in Swedish and English: Fortunes told. We could hear the beat of a drum coming from inside.

"Ooh, do you want to go in?" asked Amarjeet.

"Not really," I said. For some reason my heart took a little jump.

"Hey, there you are," said Jasper joining us. "We're supposed to head back soon."

"Five more minutes," said Amarjeet, digging in her pack for money.

"No time," I said, pulling her away from the tent. Then the drumming stopped.

A woman burst from the tent and cut a deliberate path toward us. My heart flipped again. She was dressed in strange old-fashioned clothing and there was something about her sweater and hat that made me think of the North Pole. Her dark hair and complexion glowed under the park lights as sweat dripped from her forehead.

The three of us froze as she came toward us. Then she reached over and grabbed my arm in an iron grip.

"Your life is growing harder," she began. Her accent wasn't lilting and light. She spat her words out as if they were leaving a dreadful taste in her mouth. "You must prepare yourself for a great change. Dark obstacles loom in your future as the otherworld's forces gather. I must warn you."

With all my might I tried yanking my arm from her grasp, my heart pounding in my throat.

"Child, the fates have turned against you," she said in a hollow voice. "When a rainbow of light spans the heavens, the next day you will drown."

Amarjeet gasped, and Jasper tried pulling me away. But I couldn't move or utter a sound as her words rattled in my ears.

"You must gain magic to battle the fates." She thrust a knotted rope into my jacket pocket. "Use this rope when the time comes. It can unlock nature's darkest power."

She shook her head vigorously, her dark hair flinging about. "But each time you succeed, worse will wait." Then her eyes rolled back into her head, leaving only slits of white.

CHAPTER 12

THE JOURNEY DARKENS

The creepy fortune-teller kept me in her grip, and I was paralyzed. My eyes blurred as dark shadows crept in and settled over the amusement park. The squeal of the rides and clamour of the crowd first hushed then thrummed in an eerie whine. The calliope from the carousel piped out a nursery tune that now sounded more like a funeral march.

The fortune-teller's eyes snapped back into focus, and I tugged my arm free, falling back against Jasper.

"Let's get out of here," he said. "Fast."

A crowd had gathered around us, and for a moment the fortune-teller seemed confused. Spotting me, she fastened her gaze with ferocious intent.

"Do not let the fates decide," her otherworldly voice pronounced. Then with a swish of her felt skirts, she turned and drifted back to the tent.

"What was that about?" Amarjeet said in alarm.

But before I could answer, I felt a light tap on my shoulder. In front of me stood a young man, maybe a senior in school.

He said in English, "That woman is a Sámi shaman from Lapland. I know she just gave you a fright, but be careful. Shamans have uncanny powers, including second sight."

Shaken, I nodded and then followed my friends to the arcade zone. The sun had completely sunk in the horizon, and twilight devoured the ground behind me. The chill night air gnawed through my jacket making me shiver uncontrollably. We spotted our group and began rushing back to the gates to meet up with our teachers. All the while Clive and Amanda complained bitterly how we'd made them late and we'd all get into trouble, but I wasn't paying attention.

What did the shaman mean when she said I must battle the fates? I kept thinking about her strange revelation over and over again, desperately searching for some way to make it a misunderstanding. But I couldn't think of any logical explanation for what had happened, and my spirits sank deeper.

As if reading my mind, Jasper pulled me back, and we trailed behind the others. "Cat, about what she said. Remember, no one can tell the future."

Every part of me wanted to believe him. "Why here?" I whispered harshly. "I mean, she was talking about otherworldly stuff, right? But we're thousands of miles away from Grim Hill."

"Exactly." Jasper was trying to sound reassuring, but his eyes looked troubled. Then his face brightened a little. "Are you wearing your feather?"

"Always."

"Me, too. The feathers are fairy objects, and if she really does have powers, maybe she was sensing your past fairy encounters from the feathers."

That made sense. My insides unwound, and I took a deep breath. But I touched the shaman's knotted rope in my pocket. Then I laughed a little to myself. Me? Gain magical powers? She sure had the wrong sister.

With a calmer heart we rushed through the gates to where Mr. Morrows, Ms. Dreeble, and Ms. Grimmaar were waiting with Sookie. Mr. Morrows was tapping his foot impatiently, but we weren't the last group to report back, and our teachers saved their annoyance until the final stragglers came through the gates.

"If people can't report back in a timely manner, there will be no other excursions on your own," Mr. Morrows blasted the stragglers. It was as if our group's lateness had been forgotten.

"Did you see Pippi Longstocking?" I asked Sookie.

"Uh huh," she grunted as if the whole idea was boring to her. Then with more enthusiasm she said, "We went to fantasy land, too, and they have a snow queen and a witch. And Cat, did you know—"

"Yeah," I said, cutting her off. I had just wanted to hear if she had a good time, not get the entire play-by-play. "Hey, where are your glasses?"

Sookie's lip curled slightly in annoyance, but then she got a mischievous look in her eye and pulled the glasses out of her pocket. "Fine," she said as she put them on.

"We have to hurry or we'll miss the ferry back to Gamla Stan," Mr. Morrows ordered. And even though our group wasn't on his bad side, we scrambled with everyone else.

On the trip back, the harbour was jammed with other vessels, and our boat bounced on the waves. The wind cut through my jacket and I huddled between Jasper and Amarjeet. Clive and Amanda were still giving me mean looks. Zach, Mia, and Mitch hung over the ship's rail with us as we watched the city lights reflecting against the water. We disembarked, and I asked my sister, "Where are your glasses now?" If I had to keep making sure she wore them, it would undo me on this trip.

"They're gone," she said.

"Gone where?"

"They slipped off my face," Sookie said with a wicked smile, "and fell into the water."

I was about to yell at her, but then I realized there was nothing I could do about it. But still I felt angry because Mom had paid a lot of money for those glasses. And there was no way glasses just slipped off a person's face and fell over the edge of a boat, particularly when that person was much shorter than the railing.

"Oh, little one, are you giving your sister a hard time?" Ms. Grimmaar joined us. "Did you tell her how the glasses flew off in the wind?"

"I tried," Sookie said petulantly. "But I don't think Cat believes me."

"You didn't mention the wind," I said suspiciously.

"This child's had a very long day," Ms. Grimmaar explained. "All of you have. Even your teachers look exhausted."

It was true. Mr. Morrows hovered around us keeping watch, but he was losing steam. Ms. Dreeble was unusually quiet and she slumped against the wall. We walked slowly back to our hotel, and I was grateful Sookie preferred to stick with the teachers so I didn't have to see her smug expression. Just my luck that the new headmistress had taken a liking to her—now I really would be at my little sister's beck and call.

Worse, when we got back to our room, Sookie wasn't one bit tired. Instead, she sat up in our bed going on about her day and about Ms. Grimmaar and how lucky we were to have such great teachers and did we know—

"Can your sister pipe down? I need some sleep," complained Mia.

Amarjeet agreed. "Who'd have thought out of the four of us she'd be the party animal."

It was true. Sookie was wound up and showed no signs of slowing down. "Why don't you write your day down in a travel journal?" I suggested. "That way you won't forget your fun time." *And you'll finally keep quiet*, I thought.

"That's a good idea!" Sookie jumped out of bed and went to the desk. She pulled out some stationery from her suitcase and grabbed a hotel pen. Using her left-handed hook for writing, she put the pen to paper but didn't start in her usual hastily scribbled printing. She stuck her tongue out as she concentrated and laboured on her letters. "Ms. Grimmaar asked if I knew how to write, not print. This way I can practise."

Even though the light was still on there was blissful silence, and the rest of us were able to fall asleep.

There's a splash and I'm sinking deeper and deeper into a watery, icy grave. When I try to swim back up to the surface, something has got me in its grasp and, no matter how hard I kick and struggle, it won't let go. When I look beneath me, the shaman is holding my foot, her skirts and hair billowing up in the water like seaweed, and her eyes only white slits. She's pulling me down, but when I try to scream, water gushes into my mouth.

"Cat!"

I gasped and sucked in a deep breath.

"What is it with you two?" Mia said groggily. "First your sister keeps us awake chattering like a noisy squirrel, and now you don't shut up in your sleep."

"Sorry," I sputtered and turned toward her. Sookie had tangled herself up in all the covers again. "What was I saying?"

"'It's got me,' over and over. Trust me, if I don't get some sleep, I'll get you myself." Mia turned away.

Still shivering, I huddled under the covers. But it was a long time before they warmed me up.

CHAPTER 13

A CHILLY GREETING

As we left Stockholm, our train was shrouded in silence. The chilling fog that had settled outside dampened our enthusiasm. When we stared out the windows we could only see a blur of white, and the clanging of the rails was the only sound as our train left the city behind.

I sighed wearily and rubbed my eyes. Usually my dreams had evaporated by the light of day, but not this time. The fright of it lingered and I couldn't get rid of a hollowness in my stomach. It reminded me of a feeling I'd had before: like I was hungry, but nothing seemed appetizing.

Slowly the fog lifted and we sped west from Stockholm toward our destination, the town of Blakulla. Ms. Grimmaar stood at the front of the train's car and explained what we were seeing out the windows. Sookie sat right beside her, which was fine by me. Maybe there were benefits of her being the headmistress's pet.

"We are travelling west along the Göta Canal," Ms. Grimmaar said in her sing-song accent. "This canal links the Baltic Sea to the Northern Sea, and here you will see some of the most beautiful scenery in Sweden. It will change dramatically as we leave the pastoral farmlands and travel north to wilder troll country."

Some people said "cool," and Sookie squealed in delight. Just as our spirits were beginning to rise, Mr. Morrows jumped up from his seat to seize what he called a "teaching opportunity."

"The canal was built in the early nineteenth century. Why do you suppose Sweden wanted a huge canal?" Mr. Morrows quizzed us.

Everyone shuffled uncomfortably in their seats and stayed silent. Mitch pulled his baseball cap over his face as if it would make him disappear. Mia twisted a strand of her red hair and furrowed her brow, pretending to be deep in thought so the teachers would leave her to it. Jasper probably knew the answer, but he wasn't a show off, unlike—

"Yes, Clive?" Mr. Morrows seemed relieved. It occurred to me that maybe our teacher was trying to impress the exchange school's headmistress. I looked at Clive.

"That would have been after the Industrial Revolution," Clive began. He was all about the Industrial Revolution.

"Right," Mr. Morrows said encouragingly . . . or was it desperately?

"So there would have been lots of mining going on and no trucks or even trains. Water would be the best way for transporting resources."

"Also the cheapest way," Mr. Morrows beamed.

"Did the trolls do the mining?" Sookie chirped.

Everyone burst out laughing, but not in a kind way. My face burned. But then Ms. Grimmaar came to the rescue.

"No, little one, that would be dwarves. They love to mine. But you are onto some of our Swedish legends," she said, winking at my sister. "Trolls are much lazier and steal all the silver and gold they can get their hands on." Then Ms. Grimmaar said in a serious tone, although she had a slight smirk on her face, "Trolls are stupid, nasty, ugly creatures and they are also dangerous, especially the water trolls. You must watch out for them." Her mouth twitched back a smile.

There was a round of chuckles as Sookie's eyes grew wide as saucers. Clive turned to me with a strange look of enjoyment as he watched my embarrassment. What was going on with him? Sometimes he seemed so friendly, but other times he acted like such a jerk.

Once Ms. Grimmaar had wrestled the teaching moment away from Mr. Morrows, we all began to relax and enjoy the fantastic scenery. The snow had mostly melted, and I gazed out at the tributaries and rivers and rolling hills.

By the time we approached Lake Vättern, it felt like we'd journeyed from Stockholm to another country in another time. Old Viking fortresses and castles scattered the forested landscape. Gradually, the trees gave way when the train pulled into Vadstena. The town had a gigantic castle on the lake's edge with strange rounded domes and weathered grey stone. It looked like the kind of place that would be filled with torture chambers.

"This is where we switch trains and head north," announced Ms. Grimmaar. A few of us groaned as we'd been on the train for almost two hours. But she said, "I'm sure the amazing lunch we have planned for the end of your journey will cheer you up."

Once we had switched trains and were chugging our way north, the pastures and farmland gave way to even more brooding dark forests. Craggy, jagged mountains shot up in spikes, and some of them had odd little cable cars that Ms. Grimmaar called "funiculars." The countryside seemed strange and unsettling, and the hollowness in my stomach returned.

When we finally arrived in Blakulla, the first thing I noticed was its namesake. The mountain rose forebodingly over the town, a spiked blue shadow, crooked like a cruel beckoning finger. There was no way I was going near the place. We left the train station and walked through the narrow medieval streets where flags hung from the windows above us. A local hotel on the lake's edge had set up a traditional Swedish smorgasbord for our lunch. My stomach was feeling a lot better and my mouth watered at the idea.

"Let your sister sit with the teachers," advised Mia. "Let's grab a table for the rest of us." I agreed but felt a little guilty when Sookie wandered my way and saw I hadn't left her a seat. She stared at me for a second, shrugged her shoulders, and went to join the teachers.

We sat near a window that looked over a misty lake. It was filled with tiny islands and went on so far you couldn't see the shore on the other side. As my eye swept past the town, the landscape grew eerie. I hugged myself and tried not to shiver.

"It is drafty here," complained Amarjeet. She wound her thick scarf around her neck. "But I don't want to give up the view." Soon Mitch and Jasper joined us by pulling up their table, and so did Clive. When Amanda and Zach pulled their table next to ours, Clive's face puckered into a frown. I got the feeling he wasn't crazy about Zach, but why? Unlike Clive, Zach was nice to everyone.

We were about to dig into salads, ham, deviled eggs, shrimp—the dishes went on forever! Mia and I had even helped ourselves to delicious smelling coffee. "I'm so glad there are no parents here to tell us we're too young for coffee," Mia said.

Just as I sat down, Ms. Dreeble came over.

"Your aunt has arrived," she said.

I pulled back my chair and followed Ms. Dreeble and a subdued Sookie through the tapestried halls into the ancient and stuffy-smelling hotel lobby.

Aunt Hildegaard was nothing like I had expected.

The other ladies I knew who were that age—the Greystone sisters—were slim, grey haired, and proper looking, wearing silk tea dresses and gloves and hats when they went outside. Aunt Hildegaard, tall and broad shouldered, looked extremely fit in her farming boots and thick wool sweater. Her salt-and-pepper hair was piled high on her head in braids, and her sharp green eyes sent chills down my spine. The wrinkles of her leathery face folded deeply into a stern expression.

"Hello," I said nervously.

"*God dag.*" Her large calloused hands reached out and shook ours in a hearty grip. "It's time for you to learn a few Swedish phrases." Then without so much as an "I'm so happy to see you," she turned abruptly and started talking to Ms. Dreeble.

Mom had said Aunt Hildegaard was kindly and warm, but this woman seemed neither. She appeared so—

"Formidable, isn't she?" Sookie whispered to me, shaking her head. "Mom didn't mention that. I don't want to go with her, Cat. I want to stay with the teachers." She sounded more like a little kid than usual, but she wasn't the only one who wanted to stay behind.

"They were just sitting down to lunch," Ms. Dreeble said.

"We need to get back to the farm," said our aunt. "There's a lot of work going on now that it's spring. There are livestock to herd and feed, and I'm in the middle of planting. I need extra hands today."

Work? I thought miserably as I pictured Mia sipping her coffee. My friends were probably stuffing shrimp down their throats this very moment. My stomach growled.

Ms. Grimmaar joined us. "I've enjoyed meeting your nieces, and I hope you will allow Sookie to accompany us on many of our excursions. They're both welcome to stay with me if you'd like. I live close to the school."

My heart soared with hope.

My aunt said something sharp in Swedish, and Ms. Grimmaar got a distasteful look on her face, but she quickly smiled and said, "Of course, whatever is most convenient for you."

"I want to stay," Sookie whined.

Ms. Dreeble shot us a sympathetic look and quietly said, "I'm sure you'll have a lovely time with your aunt."

It wasn't like Ms. Dreeble to lie. Then she said almost urgently, "Really, I think it's for the best."

"There's no time for nonsense girl," my aunt said briskly to Sookie. "We have to get going."

Sookie got her stubborn look, and I knew there was no way to get her on board. Then Aunt Hildegaard said, "We have to get the reindeer fed."

"You have *reindeer*?" Sookie did a full turn and grabbed my aunt's hand. "Let's get going."

My aunt hoisted Sookie's suitcase over her shoulder

and they began walking away, leaving me standing in the lobby.

My feet didn't want to move.

CHAPTER 14

A MYSTERIOUS VISITOR

"Come, Caitlin, I haven't got all day," my aunt said.

"My *name* is Cat."

Aunt Hildegaard turned sharply and fastened me with a cold, searching stare. "Cat?"

"It's short for Caitlin," Sookie volunteered.

"Well, come along, Cat." Aunt Hildegaard took off with a purposeful stride, and Sookie had a hard time keeping up. Sighing, I grabbed my suitcase and dragged it behind me. Staying with this person was definitely not one of Mom's better ideas.

Piling our suitcases in the back of an old-fashioned black truck, we climbed into the worn leather seats in the front cab. Aunt Hildegaard shifted grinding gears, and the truck lurched onto the road that followed the lake's edge out of town. Crossing several bridges, I noticed how the boiling water rushing beneath made our town's river look like a peaceful stream. Waterfalls wound through grey rock cropping ahead in the road. Turning away from that road, we travelled through a dark forested lane until we wound up a narrow path and approached a wide pasture by the lakeshore.

Beside the pasture sat a large red cabin. Between the cabin and the trees was a barn and outside that were chicken coops and a small pigpen. My aunt's farm sprawled across a narrow strip of land hemmed in by the forest on one side and the lake on the other side.

"Look!" Sookie's shriek made me jump.

"Good heavens!" said Aunt Hildegaard as she parked the truck.

"I see a reindeer!" Sookie shouted excitedly, paying no attention. She shot out the door and ran across the field.

"That girl should be more cautious approaching the animals," my aunt warned. "At least the *ren* she's headed for is docile."

"Her name is Sookie," I couldn't help mentioning.

My aunt fastened me with another serious stare and said, "Tell Sookie to come in and wash up. I'm sure you both want lunch before you begin the chores."

How could Mom do this to us? I fumed, trudging across a muddy pasture to fetch my sister. *She's hired us out as farmhands for what was supposed to be a fun trip.* Suddenly I wasn't so sure about leaving Sookie here to fend for herself when I was with the rest of the group. But my heart ached to be with my friends, and I wouldn't be able to join them again until Monday morning. Instead, I'd be stuck slaving away here for two whole days.

"Cat," Sookie's voice brimmed with excitement, "do you think this one is Rudolph? His nose is kind of pink." She was on her tiptoes and had to reach up high to put her arm around a reindeer's neck.

"Maybe you shouldn't get so close," I said from a distance. "Those reindeer are pretty big. Aunt Hildegaard said you should be careful about the animals. She also said it was time for lunch."

Sookie made a face and said, "Rudolph doesn't mind. And Aunt Hildegaard is crabby." Then after giving Rudolph a firm pat on the side of the head, she left him and came with me back to the cabin.

"What's for *middag*?" Sookie asked cheekily.

Aunt Hildegaard regarded her with a peculiar look and simply said, "You'll see soon enough. Wash up; the sink is down the hall."

I followed Sookie down the whitewashed hallway, noticing that some of the walls were birch like the floor. The windows were small, but a door at the end of the hall led to a closed-in porch with a panoramic lake view. Except for a few braided rugs, there weren't any decorations. The only furniture was a couch and rocking chair around the potbellied stove, and a birch table and chairs that had been scrubbed to a gleaming polish, just like the floors. I didn't see any televisions or computers. But I did notice the smell of fresh pine, like a house at Christmastime, combined with the sharp, fresh tang that drifted up from the lake.

After washing, we sat down at the table. Aunt Hildegaard coldly announced, "These are the rules. Sookie, you will fetch the eggs and feed the animals. Cat, you will help with the more physical chores of baling hay and planting the field."

Sookie frowned, then said, "Can I herd the reindeer?"

My aunt shook her head. "You will not enter the reindeer pen," she said, staring directly at Sookie. "You may sit on the fence and feed them grass."

Looking at us both, she continued, "You will ask permission before leaving the farm, and you will never leave the paths. Do not cross any footbridges in the area, but if you must, use utmost caution. Hold tight onto the rails and watch out below; the rivers beneath are treacherous. And you'll stay out of the forest."

Aunt Hildegaard put a plate of dark brown bread, sliced tomatoes, and pickled herring in front of us.

"Ewww," said Sookie looking at our lunch of pickled herring. I kicked her not-so-gently under the table.

"Ow, Cat."

"What's wrong?" Our aunt gave us a side glance, which seemed to size us up. I didn't think we were measuring up too well.

There was an awkward silence on our part, then Sookie blurted, "I don't like this kind of food."

"What kind of food do you like?" Aunt Hildegaard said this matter-of-factly, but she didn't sound pleased.

"Do you have frosty oats?" Sookie asked hopefully.

"No."

Sookie tried again. "Peanut butter?"

"No."

Finally, Sookie said, "Jam?"

Aunt Hildegaard left the table and came back with a jar labelled *lingonberry* that had purple stuff inside. I held my breath, worrying what Sookie would say next. She dug in her knife, then plopped an indelicate amount of the purple jam on her bread and smeared it to the edges. She bit in and declared, "Not bad."

"What about you?" Aunt Hildegaard stared at me again, her mouth not flinching toward a smile or a frown.

"I'm fine, thank you," I replied, making sure my own mouth didn't move. I skipped the herring but put the tomatoes onto my bread. Tomatoes weren't my favourite, but I didn't want my aunt to think Sookie and I were spoiled kids. Once again I thought of my friends, now finishing off their giant smorgasbord. My aunt left the table again and brought us two glasses of cold milk.

"Cat prefers coffee," Sookie said.

My eyes widened, and then almost popped out of my head, when my aunt took a pot off the stove and poured that forbidden liquid into a cup. I grabbed my glass, dumped milk into the black brew, and took a delicate sip. Wincing, I spooned in some honey she'd brought to the table. *Not bad at all, Sookie*, I thought. She had definitely scored some points.

Aunt Hildegaard dropped into a chair and took a sip from her own cup. The way she sat rigidly in her chair gave me the sense she wasn't much for relaxing. "Tell me," said Aunt Hildegaard, "how is your mother?"

The question caught me off guard, and for a moment I couldn't think of what to say. Funny, nobody had ever asked me that before. I could say straight away how I was doing, or even most of my friends. I could maybe even take a shot at my sister. But my *mom*?

I guessed she liked her night school courses because it was going to get us ahead, and she told us how lucky she was that her work hours fit into our schedules. I knew she didn't like stretching money to make ends meet . . . and that's what got me into this mess.

"She's fine," was all I said.

"Well then, time for work." My aunt took our cups and put them into the sink, even though I hadn't finished my coffee. Sighing, I began clearing the table.

The sun was low on the horizon when we'd finally finished washing the dinner dishes and putting them away. My muscles ached from throwing hay in the barn, and my back didn't want to bend ever again after I'd helped plant turnips.

"Hey, Cat, do you think Santa Claus lives across this lake?"

I shrugged my shoulders. Who was I to say where Santa Claus lives?

Sookie had spent her day gathering eggs from the chicken coop, and Aunt Hildegaard had taught her how to milk a cow. At every free second, she stole off to the pasture next to the lake and climbed the fence to feed handfuls of grass to the reindeer.

"Sookie," my Aunt snapped, "what is this creature doing in my house?"

After dinner Sookie had lugged a big black cat into the cabin, and I had simply thought it was my aunt's pet. She'd poured the cat a bowl of milk on the sunporch, and now it had wandered into the kitchen looking for more.

"She was hungry," Sookie said. "Can she stay inside? She really likes me."

"Certainly not," my aunt said. "I've never seen that beast. Who knows where it's been."

Before there was a showdown, I reached for the cat, but it hissed menacingly and arched its back.

"Hey, I'm a Cat, too." But I couldn't go near the wild thing. Instead Sookie reached over and slung the cat over her shoulders like a sack of potatoes and took it to the door.

"It's not too cold in the barn," she consoled it, then shut the door.

I hung the checkered dishcloth on the rack and sat wearily on a chair, wondering what my friends were doing now. Even though I'd finished dinner—the tiny boiled potatoes, meatballs, and delicious gingerbread for dessert were a step up from lunch—I still had this empty feeling in my stomach.

All at once I remembered when I'd had that feeling before. It was after my dad had left, and we'd moved to our new town. Mom had explained how I was homesick for my old life. Now I was homesick for my new life. I suppose that was an improvement.

There was a timid knock, and when my aunt opened the kitchen door, freezing night air flooded the cabin. My heart jumped as a sickly grey hand reached through the crack of the door, its long fingers curled menacingly around a tin cup. Then Aunt Hildegaard did something peculiar. She went to the fridge, brought out the milk, and began filling the battered cup.

My stomach lurched when I noticed the hand was missing a finger! As my aunt poured the milk to the brim, Sookie and I crowded the door to get a better look. The man in the shadows wore a hat that wrapped around his neck like a scarf, partly covering his long grey hair and beard. He had on an oversized dark coat, and his boots reached up to his knees. His features were craggy and sharp, and he had beady eyes and the strangest nose I'd ever seen. I forced myself to look away and stop staring.

After the man got his milk, he silently left the porch.

"That is Osgaard," said my aunt. "He is my reindeer herder and helps out with the farm."

When my aunt shut the door, she almost fell over the black cat, which had snuck back inside. Sookie grabbed the animal and headed for the door again. I followed and became chillingly aware of a sense of foreboding. My feather, tucked under my shirt, was heating up as if I'd slipped a hot water bottle next to my skin. We watched the reindeer herder move toward the shadows as the cat ran from the porch.

"Cat," Sookie whispered, "do you think he's one of Santa's elves?"

"No," I said to my sister. "Not even close."

CHAPTER 15

AN EERIE INCIDENT

There was something just not right about my aunt's farm. I couldn't shake my uneasiness the next day as I went through my chores and tried to keep an eye on my sister. Sookie was always asking the wrong questions to our aunt, like, "Why can't the cat come in? Why can't I play with the reindeer? Why can't I swim in the lake? Why can't we take the boat out? Why can't I . . ."

Worse, by the afternoon, Sookie refused to mind our aunt, and she kept sneaking away to play with the cat or reindeer. I was doing my best by checking up on her constantly. That's why I'd forgotten the full milk jug inside the barn.

I'd just finished pouring the milk from the bucket into a hefty earthenware jug to bring back to the house for the next morning's breakfast. The crimson sun was setting in a hazy red horizon when the hair on the back of my neck prickled. With a growing urgency I thought, *I should make sure Sookie's inside the cabin.*

I ran for the cabin and asked, "Is Sookie here?"

Aunt Hildegaard was knitting by the warm stove and muttering to herself, "Be wary of the fog." Finally, she looked up from her needles and wool and acknowledged me. "She's been playing on the sun porch."

But when I checked, Sookie wasn't there. Quickly, I rushed back outside and found my sister with that stupid black cat by the lake. There was a grey fog rolling in from the water, its creeping tendrils ready to snatch any passersby.

"Time to come in," I urged, "before you get scratched." Once again, the cat arched its back and began hissing when I approached. I figured the huge animal could do a lot of damage.

"She likes me," Sookie said, "and I like her." She looked smug, as if to say, *so if she rips you up into shreds, that's your fault.*

I backed away as the cat shot out a clawed paw and said, "Well, get back inside before Aunt Hildegaard discovers you're not there. Play with the cat in the morning."

Sookie sighed dramatically and embraced the cat, taking her life into her own hands if you asked me. We were almost back to the cabin when I remembered the milk jug. So after Sookie went inside, I headed back to the barn to fetch the milk.

As I walked back up to the house, chills crept up and down my spine. I hurried past a huge pile of rocks half hidden in shadow. Then I saw something that almost made me drop the jug of milk. That pile of rocks in the yard slowly started to move, morphing into the shadowy reindeer herder.

He stood right in front of me. My heart slammed against my chest as I froze and watched him pull his battered tin cup from a brown sack. He held the cup out to me.

Hoisting the jug to pour the milk, I tried to control my shaking hands that were sloshing milk on the ground before I could fill the cup. I tried not to stare at his strangely deformed hand or his hideous warty skin. As he drank the milk, I rushed for the cabin clutching the heavy pitcher to my chest, debating whether or not to drop the jug as I fled. *Don't be a baby*, I thought. Behind me I heard loud lapping sounds, as if the cat had crept up and began drinking the spilled milk. But I couldn't force myself to turn around. I was too frightened by the crazy idea that Osgaard was on his hands and knees, licking the ground with a long black tongue.

Slamming the door behind me, I sucked in a ragged breath.

"Good heavens!" These seemed to be Aunt Hildegaard's favourite words. "There's no need to slam the door."

"Sorry," I muttered, putting the jug in the fridge.

"Did you bring the milk pail with you?" asked Aunt Hildegaard. "I need to wash it out for the morning."

I tried thinking of an excuse not to go outside again; somehow I didn't think Aunt Hildegaard would think too favourably of, "I'm scared." Instead, I settled with, "I'm tired. Can I get it in the morning?"

"Certainly not," my aunt said brusquely. "Firstly, you are giving the bacteria plenty of time to multiply instead of cleaning the pail thoroughly right away. We don't leave things dirty. Secondly," she eyed me in that way again, as if Mom had been dragging us up instead of bringing us up properly, "never put off until tomorrow what can be done today."

Panicky thoughts darted through my mind. Which would be less terrifying: walking slowly to the barn and keeping a sharp eye out for Osgaard, or just running for it, not looking left or right? I opened the door, shut it behind me carefully, and made a dash for the barn, keeping my eyes fastened on its entrance. But as I neared the barn, I swore I could hear voices. I slammed to a stop outside the door.

Whoever they were, they seemed angry—but the argument was in Swedish. I hadn't seen anyone else working on this farm, so who exactly was Osgaard arguing with? Or was it even Osgaard? I'd never heard him speak. Deciding to make a lot of noise to announce my arrival, I began whistling and humming as loudly as I could. The arguing stopped, and I heard footsteps heading from the other side of the barn into the forest. Good. I opened the door with, as Sookie would say, more than a little trepidation and stepped inside the damp, smelly barn. Aunt Hildegaard was a meticulous farmer, scrubbing the cow's stall daily, but I decided nothing was less enchanting than the smell of old, wet hay. I ran for the milk pail.

When I passed through the door I heard, "Hissss."

Sitting on a rafter above me was the black cat.

"Nice kitty," I gulped, thinking at any moment it would leap from the rafter and slide its nasty claws across my scalp and down my back. I kept a wary eye up above. That cat had a menacing stare.

"Hissss."

Its wide-open mouth revealed the longest fangs I'd ever seen. All pointy and sharp and directed at me. Carefully, I started backing away toward the cabin. What was Sookie thinking playing with such a nasty beast? It was practically the size of a lynx. The cat leaped at me.

Spinning around, I made a run for it. I didn't look back. Not even after I tossed the milk pail in the sink, and Aunt Hildegaard repeated, "Good heavens." Not even as Sookie kept singing an eerie song as she stared out the window into the fog. Instead, I threw on my pajamas and dived under my quilt.

Once my heart settled, I said, "I think you should stay away from that cat, Sookie. It might turn on you. It's big enough to give you a horrible bite or scratch."

"She's a nice animal." Then Sookie giggled, "You're the scaredy cat."

Shamed into silence, I tossed and turned all night, waking from the unsettling ghostly sighs of the wind as it blew through the cracks in the window frame.

Sookie spent Sunday tromping around in her boots, chasing chickens, and playing with the stupid cat. She was having a great time and didn't seem to mind our aunt's disapproval one bit. And she also appeared completely unaware of the farm's eeriness: of the odd sounds, peculiar shadows and mists, or the strange reindeer herder whom we only saw at night. Maybe it was because she was too busy being a pain.

"You better get that cat out of here," I said before dinner.

Sookie had snuck the cat onto the sun porch again.

"She's cold. And she doesn't like the barn."

"Right," I said shaking my head. "Well, too bad. She'd better settle for the barn before Aunt Hildegaard sees her and gets angry."

"Humph," Sookie said. The cat hissed at me again, and I stepped back.

"Cat, she knows you don't like her; that's the problem," Sookie said, stroking the cat's head.

"Hey," I said, "the cat started it." I swear, it looked like the cat's lips curled into a grin.

"Wash up for dinner," our aunt ordered. "And Sookie, it is your job to set the table."

Sookie quickly opened the sliding glass door and shooed away the cat. Sighing, she went into the kitchen. Unlike Mom, our aunt didn't let Sookie get away with skipping chores.

Later that night I stumbled exhausted into bed again. Sookie was already snoring in the bed next to mine, tucked under a matching quilt of tiny leaves and red berries. I was having a hard time getting used to the strange nighttime noises; the wind's gasps in the loneliest hours was making me shiver and pull my quilt close. At least being sleepless meant I wasn't having nightmares. But then I heard a different sound. It was as if something was scratching at our window.

First I kept the quilt over my head, willing the sound to stop. It was as if branches of a tree were scritch-scratching against the glass, but I knew there were no trees outside our bedroom window. Finally, when the noise didn't stop, I forced myself to take a look.

My throat closed in as my gaze fixed upon two yellow ghostly eyes that had cat-like black slits in the centre. The shadowy face pressed against the frosted glass pane. I choked back a scream, but still let out a quiet yelp. Sitting up fast, I ran to the window, but by the time I got there, the horrific face had disappeared. I yanked the curtains shut.

"Sookie, did you see—?" I gasped, but Sookie lay in her bed cocooned under her quilt, fast asleep.

Should I wake up Aunt Hildegaard? Clearly someone was outside spying on us. The problem was, how would I describe what I saw? How could I explain that whoever was peering through my window *wasn't human*?

My aunt didn't seem like the patient type or exactly trusting of my judgment. It would have to wait until morning, when I could talk to the only other person who might understand: Jasper.

CHAPTER 16

A LOGICAL EXPLANATION

Early Monday morning, my aunt dropped me off at Svartberg Academy. Fortunately, I still had jet lag, otherwise Sookie and I would never have survived farm time. Aunt Hildegaard stopped the truck at the edge of town in front of the old school building. Its steep, sloping roof and tiny windows were crouched under birch trees studded with green leaf buds.

When my aunt had said the school was called a *gymnasieskolan*, I got my hopes up that we'd be doing nothing but P.E. because that sounded like "gymnasium." Sadly, that wasn't the case at all. It was just the word for "high school" in Swedish.

Our headmistress, Ms. Grimmaar, greeted us and she asked me, "Where is your adorable little sister? Didn't she come with you today?"

I said, "No," and Ms. Grimmaar seemed disappointed. "I was planning a lovely field trip for this morning, but I suppose it can be postponed while Ms. Dreeble contacts your aunt. Perhaps your sister will be able to join us later in the day."

Great, I thought. Sookie had driven me crazy over the weekend. Now Ms. Grimmaar wanted Sookie to tag along at school events as well. So instead of the field trip in the morning, we had our first language class to learn phrases in Swedish. *Behaga, tack,* ("please," "thank you,") we'd droned for the twentieth time.

Ursakta mig was "excuse me," but when the guys practised that one, they all felt compelled to belch first. Hilarity reigned, and it seemed Mr. Morrows didn't have the energy to shout at us.

As things got out of control, Anne Britt paired us off with Swedish students so we could help them with their English. But they were a lot better at English than we were at Swedish, and we mostly just chatted with them, not that they seemed interested. The problem was, Swedish secondary school was like our senior high. All the students were older—like Anne Britt, who couldn't have been less interested in hanging with us and kept rolling her eyes. At break, my friends and I huddled together in the long white corridor outside the classrooms.

"Why do you think we're on exchange with this school?" asked Amarjeet. "Why not billet us with students the same age?"

Mia shrugged her shoulders, "Maybe because this is a private school?"

Clive fired Mia a scornful look. "Why would that matter?"

"Well, maybe they don't usually do international school exchanges," Mia said, "and didn't realize there would be a big age difference between our two high schools."

Clive opened his mouth and shut it again when he realized it had to be something like that. I wondered myself how Svartberg students would even fit in our desks when they came in the fall. Score one for Mia.

While everyone else continued complaining about the age difference, I pulled Jasper away.

"Jasper," I began, "weird things are happening on my aunt's farm."

Jasper's eyes widened. "What kind of things?"

I told him about the wraith-like mist that had rolled off the lake, the creepy reindeer herder, and the malevolent face I'd seen spying through my bedroom window. "Those eyes were pure evil," I finished.

"What about your feather. Has it, um, reacted?" Jasper asked.

"Considering it practically scorched me a few times, I'd say yes."

"Funny," said Jasper, "mine has been glowing as well this weekend, especially late at night." He frowned. "I thought it was suspicious when Mr. Morrows and Ms. Dreeble just sat in our hotel lobby drinking coffee all day and staring out at that mist on the lake. We had the run of the town."

"No," I said, utterly envious. I'd missed so much fun! "How did you get away with that? Mr. Morrows and Ms. Dreeble had a ton of work planned for us."

"I know, it's not like them one bit." Jasper frowned with concern. "Maybe they're just jet lagged?" And it suddenly occurred to me that such a dramatic change in time and location could have affected me as well.

"Maybe I've been seeing things because my sleep pattern is all messed up. Plus, I'll admit my experiences with fairy spells have left me a little paranoid. After all, this place is no Grim Hill."

"Possibly." Jasper ran his hand through his hair, which he no longer spiked. Instead of using gel, he now tousled it with wax. Since his transformation from bookworm to sports star, he was careful to keep his hair trendy. "Always look for the simplest explanation."

I was glad Jasper hadn't changed on the inside; he was as good a source of information as an encyclopedia. "But," I added, "living in our town, sometimes the simplest explanation has to include what most people see as unbelievable: magic."

"Right. Just in case, I'll pull a little research in the library on this part of Sweden."

I nodded. "Not to mention, there's still the problem of my aunt. She's kind of peculiar," I whispered.

"How so?" Jasper did the thing with his hair again.

"She's cold and unfriendly." I shook my head. "I don't understand. She was the one who wanted both of us to come to Sweden. She told my mom that she wanted to see her grandnieces, but I swear, it seems we're just an annoyance."

"It's because of her age," Clive's voice came from behind.

With a flash of irritation, I spun around. How much had Clive eavesdropped? What had he overheard?

"What do you mean?" I asked.

"When you live with an older person like my gran," Clive began explaining, "you've got to realize that she comes from a different era."

"Uh huh," I said, waiting for Clive to make some sense.

"When Skeeter and I had come to stay with our gran, we had to make a lot of changes."

I saw a sadness settle across Clive's face and I realized that I'd never thought about what had happened to his parents until now.

"We made way too much noise, we didn't listen properly, and we fooled around too much," explained Clive. "At first I thought it wasn't fair how my gran seemed disappointed with us all the time."

It was as if Clive was explaining exactly how I felt about my aunt.

"Then I realized," said Clive, "my gran had grown up with a lot more discipline and rules about behaviour. That's how she measured us, and it wasn't really that she was unkind or unhappy with us, but that she had a different set of expectations."

I wondered if that was my aunt's problem. The Greystone sisters weren't like that and they were older. *But*, said my inner voice, *we only visited them from time to time. We weren't constantly underfoot.*

"So how did you work things out with your grandmother?"

"I made sure Skeeter and I toed the line," Clive said matter-of-factly. "Besides, it was for the best. Inner discipline gives you a big advantage in sports and school."

And turns you into an impatient, arrogant, unkind . . . Then I realized that explained a lot about Clive, why he seemed more like a strict adult than like one of us.

"Thanks for the tip," I said. "So I just have to realize my aunt's expectations are for Sookie and me to be hard working and obedient."

"Just remember those old-fashioned sayings," explained Clive. "Children should be seen and not heard; spare the rod, spoil the child." Then with an evil grin he added, "Girls are sugar and spice and everything nice, and the man is in charge."

"Yeah, right," I shook my head. So that's why Clive always acted as if he'd stepped out of a time warp. Jasper stifled a laugh. Even though I couldn't see myself ever agreeing with all that stuff, maybe he was right about my aunt.

A sudden commotion down the corridor next to the biggest classroom made me forget about my aunt and her strange farm. Ms. Grimmaar and Ms. Dreeble were back and they'd brought Sookie. And by the sounds of the complaints, some students didn't appreciate it.

I rushed to where students and teachers gathered. Pointing at Sookie, one of the older Swedish boys leaned over to his friends and said not-so-quietly, "Bad enough we get a pack of kiddies to take care of. Now we've become a daycare."

Sookie stuck out her tongue at him, making the older students grumble even more.

"And you'd better teach your sister who's the boss," Clive said.

I sighed. "It's not like Skeeter always listens."

Clive had that cocky look on his face that I so disliked. "He listens to me at home. You'd do best to make sure your sister does the same and doesn't act like a brat."

"Hey," I said sharply, "Sookie's not a brat."

I stormed into class and stopped next to the teacher's desk just in time to catch my sister tattling.

"Ms. Grimmaar, that boy is mean."

The headmistress quickly dismissed the boy from the room, saying sharply, "You will not be the tour guide today." Sookie looked smug.

Clive shook his head. Okay, maybe Sookie could be a little bratty, but only I was allowed to say it.

"Today, Darkmont students, you are in for a wonderful tour," Ms. Grimmaar explained enthusiastically. "We will be going to Gamla Stan."

"Isn't that in Stockholm?" asked Amarjeet. *Right. That was where Sookie and I had gotten lost*, I remembered.

Ms. Grimmaar smiled and said, "'Gamla Stan' means 'old town,' and that is what I have planned for today. We will be doing a historical walk through the medieval section of the town." Mr. Morrows and Ms. Dreeble didn't say anything; for some reason they looked exhausted, but they nodded even as their eyes seemed to glaze over.

When we walked outside the school, a queer fog rolled in from the lake. Mr. Morrows and Ms. Dreeble seemed to slump from exhaustion.

Ms. Grimmaar ploughed ahead with our plans, but a sinking feeling told me that Jasper was right. It wasn't just my aunt's farm; there was definitely something weird going on in this town.

CHAPTER 17

THE WITCHING YEARS

We made our way down the narrow cobbled streets of the old town. The low stone buildings with dark, tiny doors made me feel like I should be wearing a medieval gown and cape.

While most of the fog had lifted, there was still something unsettling about this part of town that I never noticed in Gamla Stan in Stockholm. It could have been the shadows that the sun couldn't penetrate, or the chilling draft as the wind worked its way through the maze of buildings, or the shivers that went up and down my arms when my jacket brushed up against both sides of the narrow alleys. Either way, the hair on the nape of my neck stood up, and goosebumps broke out all over my body.

Ms. Grimmaar beckoned us to gather at the main intersection of cross streets, where a crumbling stone statue stood at the centre of a square. Jasper and I made our way to the front to get a better look at the statue.

"Gruesome," Sookie said admiringly.

The statue showed a woman in a long cloak and a towering witch's hat. She had a wicked-looking troll on a chain. When I counted the fingers on the troll's hand, there were only three! I couldn't help but think of when I'd seen a hand like that before. But the grimacing, hideous face of the troll looked purely inhuman, not like our reindeer herder.

"It was common for our ancestors to depict witches in a grotesque and fantastical way." Ms. Grimmaar had that tone Mr. Morrows used when he was rattling off historical facts. I was surprised he didn't jump right in and join her as our tour guide through the ages.

"It was a tragic time," she continued. "Often, women who were mercilessly persecuted as witches in the Middle Ages were really wise village women—valuable citizens who helped heal the sick and brought new babies into the world."

Ms. Grimmaar was right that they'd made the witch's face ugly and evil; no one looked like that. Except . . . the statue's eyes had narrow cat pupils, just like the face I had seen staring through my bedroom window.

I began shivering and sucked in a ragged breath.

"What is it?" asked Jasper.

"The simplest explanation might be that the townspeople are frightened by a real witch. Like the one I saw outside my window."

Jasper blinked several times before scratching his head and saying, "What?"

Instead of answering right away, my mind raced as I followed our tour group to a squat yellow building outside the square.

"After the accused woman was brought to the square," explained Ms. Grimmaar, "she was sent into this building for her trial. Here her accusers were given the power to declare whether or not she was a witch by simply staring at her."

"That's not fair," a few of us murmured.

A couple of the older boys laughed and made some remark in Swedish. My stomach took a dive when Sookie pointed the boys out to Ms. Grimmaar. The headmistress said something sharp, and the boys broke away from each other and came up to the front to stand beside the headmistress. They didn't look happy. All of us followed Ms. Grimmaar in a silent procession until we were on the outskirts of town, close to the towering spiked mountain of Blakulla. I hadn't realized the mountain was cut off from the town by a wide channel, and we gazed at it over the treacherous waves.

"Here was where the final part of a witch's trial took place." Ms. Grimmaar pointed to the water. "The accused woman was tied and thrown into the depths of the water. If she managed to untie herself and float to the top, the townspeople then weighted her down with heavier chains because they believed her escape proved she was a powerful witch."

I gawked at the grey thrashing waves, thinking how they were nothing but a watery graveyard for the accused women. "What made the townspeople think a person was a witch?" I broke the silence.

"Those were superstitious times. People didn't have science to explain the events around them," Ms. Grimmaar explained. Ms. Dreeble nodded weakly in agreement.

I couldn't help notice a few of the Swedish students bristled at that. A voice from the crowd spoke out. "My grandfather told me that the witches caused crops to fail and livestock and children to get sick."

"Who said that?" asked the headmistress. Sookie singled the boy out from the other students.

Ms. Grimmaar smiled kindly and it made her more attractive, as if a calming light shone inside her. With a patient voice she said, "People in those times didn't understand that malnourishment and illness were a result of the failed crops."

"Well, yeah," said the boy. "But my grandfather said—"

Ms. Grimmaar had already turned and walked away. Then several students, two boys and a girl, crouched down beside Sookie and whispered something. I noticed my sister's eyes grow huge, and when they brimmed with tears, I hurried to check on her.

"What's wrong?" I asked, glaring at the girl who'd slinked back to the middle of the group.

"They said that I'd better step away from the water because water trolls love to eat little children, especially a nasty little witch like me." Sookie sniffed as a tear trailed down her cheek.

"They were only teasing," I said. "It's best to pretend you don't care." *Way better than telling on them all the time.* It was the only way to get Sookie to stop angering the older students. What they had said to her was mean, but I was sure they didn't understand that the fairy world was not imaginary for my sister. I wanted to reassure Sookie that witches and trolls weren't real, but how could I when I was beginning to be unsure myself?

Sookie wiped the tear from her face, and I had to hand it to her for fastening the older students with a fierce look. "They're despicable," she said menacingly.

Jasper and Clive had come over to see what was wrong, and surprisingly, Clive took it upon himself to go over to those students who'd threatened Sookie. "You want to scare someone?" he shouted. "Try and scare me."

Even though the boys were taller, they backed off. I shook my head in disbelief when Clive walked back. "I thought you said Sookie was a brat, but now you're defending her."

"It's wrong to pick on someone who isn't able to fight back," Clive said. Clive did have good principles. The problem was that he expected everyone to live up to them.

Ms. Grimmaar rejoined our group. "Perhaps we've had enough gloomy tales for the day." She waved her arm at the sun, which was determined to shed a bit of warmth and light into the shroud of shadows. "Ah, children, it is turning into a bright and beautiful day. Go and enjoy the rest of the afternoon sightseeing."

We took off like a shot before Mr. Morrows or Ms. Dreeble begged to differ. I looked back only once to see Sookie engaged in a deep and rather earnest-looking conversation with the headmistress. I almost had to laugh at how serious my little sister appeared. But Ms. Grimmaar had crouched down and was listening intently to her. She made a shooing motion with her hand, granting me a gift: permission to hang out with my friends while Sookie stayed with the teachers.

As we rounded the town square, and Amarjeet, Mia, and the others ducked into a tourist shop, I held Jasper back. "Check this out with me," I said moving toward the witch statue. Pointing to the inscription at the base of the monument, I asked several bystanders, "*Ursakta mig*, but could you please, I mean *snälla*, tell me what those words mean?"

"Certainly," said a townsman in clear English. "This statue was built in the Middle Ages during the witching years that plagued our town. It's a warning: *Fair is foul, and foul is fair. Beware the reek of mystic air.*"

Jasper quickly said, "*Tack.*"

The townsman smiled and said, "*Varsagod.*" After saying "you're welcome," he mentioned something curious. "These mists that have been creeping in from the lake especially at night and early in the morning." He let out an uneasy laugh. "My grandmother would have said it's a bad sign that the witches are returning."

"You mean people are still superstitious?" Jasper asked.

"It's common folklore, especially this time of year," the man said. "Many grandmothers might say, 'Keep a close eye on old Blakulla, especially on Walpurgis Night.'"

The man raised the collar of his jacket, wrapping the scarf tighter around his neck, and hurried away.

"I wonder what Walpurgis Night is?"

Jasper said quietly, "I guess we've got some investigating to do."

I knew Jasper was right. We needed to find out what Walpurgis Night and witches had in common.

Whatever the connection was, it was already giving me a bad feeling.

CHAPTER 18

A PERILOUS PLAGUE

We'd spent another afternoon researching but hadn't found a thing. I wished I could just ask my aunt what superstitions she'd heard about; she'd lived near this town all her life. The problem was I got this uneasy sense that my aunt wasn't exactly what she appeared to be, and neither was her creepy reindeer herder.

"What's going on?" Clive asked as Jasper and I slipped out of the Svartberg library.

"What do you mean?" I asked, making my face as innocent as possible.

"You and Jasper have been sneaking off from our language classes this whole week," he said. "And on field trips into town, you two always disappear at some point."

As I wondered what to say, Jasper dropped the ball. "We're researching."

It's not exactly subterfuge, I thought, *when a person blurts the truth.*

"Researching what?" Clive asked.

"Witches," Jasper said directly, ignoring my shaking head.

Interesting: I rarely saw Clive speechless. But he totally surprised me with a minute of silence.

"There is something wrong here, isn't there?" Clive's eyes darted around the empty white corridor. Except for the three of us, every other student was inside their morning class, and the silence was oppressive.

Again, I responded cautiously. "What do you mean?"

"First," Clive held up a finger, "this is the weirdest town. Whenever we go on a field trip, it doesn't matter where we go, either to study the geography or to learn about Vikings, a strange fog rolls in from the water. Then everyone begins talking about medieval witch trials. Even our teachers!"

"I guess that's sort of unusual," I said. "But you have to admit, Mr. Morrows likes anything historical, and I have known Ms. Dreeble to care very deeply about injustice to women back in the old days."

Clive held up finger number two. "Okay, but there's something not right about a lot of the townspeople. It's as if every day they look more and more frightened. I bet if we go into town after the field trip this afternoon, there will be scarcely a soul in the streets, especially after dusk."

"Okay, we've noticed that, too." Although not quite the way Clive had. We were noticing the way our feathers glowed, and how we too sensed a growing uneasiness. Clive was actually pretty observant.

"And number three," Clive struck his third finger, "I've felt this way before, and I think it means trouble." His face grew puzzled. "Like real life and dreams get mixed up, and I can't tell which is which."

Jasper and I looked at each other. "Well," Jasper said, "for what it's worth, there have been strange things that have happened before in our town, and most people think it's just a dream. And we both think that something peculiar is going on now."

Clive stared at us and then at the empty white corridor. He wasn't the type to just let it go. "What do *you* think is happening?"

I shook my head. "We have no idea, except I do know that fog has a bad feel to it. A man on the street warned us about it, and I've seen the way people in town avoid it—going in their houses or shops until it passes. Also, I've been seeing strange, creepy things at my aunt's farm. Like a face in our window at night that had the same witch eyes as the statue in the centre of town." I shuddered. I barely slept through the weekend because I got the feeling someone had been staring in our window again. Even though I always made sure the curtains were closed, I still felt watched. "We're thinking there is something going on, and it has to do with witches."

"That's impossible," Clive said dismissively. Then he grew a shade paler. "Um, why do I think I've said that before?" He shook his head as if to dislodge a distant memory.

"It's *not* impossible," Jasper said. "Although, I can't say either way what's going on here. Our research has hit a serious snag. All the books in the library are in Swedish.

And we haven't been given a password to use the school computers." At that moment, the bell rang and the corridor grew thunderous as students spilled from the classrooms.

We dropped our conversation and followed the Darkmont crowd into the crisp afternoon sunshine as a school bus pulled up for the field trip to the lake. There was no point worrying about anything until we got back to school. Like clockwork, my aunt pulled up in her battered truck and let Sookie out on the curb.

Sookie had been attending all our field trips in the afternoon. And I was no longer furious about her tagging along; I didn't like her at the farm if I wasn't there. Besides, the first thing Sookie always did was glom onto our teachers, so it wasn't as if she was clinging to me. And since that first day in town, she'd learned to stop tattling on the other students, and they kept away from her.

We piled in the bus first. The Swedish students always hung back because they made it clear they preferred not to be associated with us. My mouth gaped when a few of the students sullenly walked past us to the back of the bus.

"Wow, what happened to them?" I twisted my head around, even though I knew better than to stare.

"Ugh," said Mia. "Is it contagious?"

"Maybe they binged on junk food," suggested Amarjeet.

"Then I'm never eating sugar again," said Mitch.

Somehow I thought whatever had splattered their faces in huge, crusty, weeping pustules had nothing to do with zits. I saw a picture of smallpox once that had terrified me, but these students didn't seem desperately ill in that way, just miserable. It wasn't lost on me that these were the students who had picked on Sookie, or that she had a smug look as they walked past her.

This wasn't good. I hunkered down on the worn leather seat of the bus and stared silently out the window as we drove to the lake. The black forests of Sweden closed in on me, smothering the light and leaving me buried in the dark. *Was Sookie practising magic again?* I felt guilty at the thought. Just because she didn't feel sorry for those pox-infested students didn't mean she caused their trouble. After all, the havoc Sookie brought with her magic was always accidental.

When we arrived at the lake, I looked out onto the sparkling water and let the brisk freshwater air lighten my heart. Several wooden boats with tall masts and dark sails bobbed on the crystal lake. Red summer cottages dotted the shore, making this place look peaceful and inviting.

That is, until Mia asked, "What's that?"

We looked to where Mia was pointing, and across the water thick white fog swirled toward the shore. The mists took the forms of wraiths, twisting like tormented ghosts.

Even the guys did a double take, and a few people gasped. We stepped back from the lake's edge as the eerie fog stretched its ghostly arms toward us. Shivers crept along my spine and hair prickled on the nape of my neck. My feather glowed hot against my skin, which didn't surprise me at all.

"What's that sound?" Amarjeet said uneasily.

We listened. A strange thrum rippled along the lakeshore and then from behind in the blackened forest. The thrumming began growing louder, as if we were standing on top of a giant heart that was waking beneath our feet. *Brumm, brumm.* The rhythm grew and the ground began to shake.

The ferns near the lake started rustling. *Brumm, brumm.* Together we all backed away from the lakeshore when the tall lake grass began shaking. *Brumm, brumm.*

Looking left and right, we couldn't see what was making the noise, but still it grew. A popping sound exploded from the rushes and again behind us from the thick ferns that carpeted the edge of the woods. Mia shrieked.

We stared wildly as an army of slimy toads hopped out from the forest and the lakeshore, and we were caught right in the middle! They were all sizes, from tiny green frogs that could leap shoulder high to the biggest, ugliest toads I'd ever seen, and I didn't mind amphibians. But they came in thousands, and they began dropping from trees onto our heads and shoulders. Everyone raced toward the bus and most of us were screaming. We had frogs plopping on top of our heads, frogs tangling in our hair, and frogs squirming down the front of our shirts!

One cold frog landed inside the collar of my jacket and began scrambling down my back. But no one heard my scream since all of us were shouting and trying to shake toads out of our clothes. As I ran, a plump toad landed on my scalp and began a slimy slide down my cheek. Would I get warts? Lots of people began tripping and falling over the frogs and toads, and I stopped and helped Amarjeet back up on her feet. Mostly, though, I just wanted to keep running.

Then I saw something that struck terror in my heart.

CHAPTER 19

A LITTLE WITCHCRAFT

Sookie's face was a mask of wickedness and she laughed uproariously as fleeing students clamoured to get into the school bus. She blocked their way until the bus driver lifted her up and carried her to a seat. Then she pasted her face to the bus window and kept on laughing.

Sookie, what have you done? I thought in a panic. Maybe she thought we looked funny scrambling and ricocheting off each other trying to jam into the bus. That's what I hoped. Except Sookie didn't have a single frog on her!

We made our way inside the bus and collapsed gratefully onto the seats. It was a long ride back, and by the time we arrived at the school, our nerves were shot. For the whole trip, the bus driver kept pulling to the side of the road as yet another series of shrieks echoed through the bus, and we'd dump the latest hitchhiking toads into the grass.

"Will you look at that," Mia whispered ominously when we finally stood outside the school.

The Swedish students filed off the bus, and I noticed more faces had broken out in seeping pustules. Red patches of bumps blotched their skin as if they'd smeared pizza all over their faces.

"No one said it was contagious," Zach said, alarmed.

"Shouldn't they be quarantined?" asked Mitch. Then more hopefully, "And the school closed?"

Clive leaned toward me, his face full of worry. "It doesn't take a genius to link frogs and pox to witchcraft. I'd still say it's all impossible, but we've got to find out what's going on. And I have a feeling it's not going to be anything I'd call logical."

He was right about that. I rubbed a hand over my face, but my skin still felt smooth under my fingertips.

"Don't worry, Cat," Sookie chirped as she scooted past me. With a nasty smirk she continued, "Only mean students will get the pox."

Relief did not pour into me. As a matter of fact, my stomach became a wretched twist of knots. I didn't need to hear what I already knew to be true, when Jasper turned to me and whispered, "Sookie is up to magic."

And this time it was even worse. The magic she was performing was meant to cause harm. She'd never done that before. *Oh, Sookie,* I thought miserably, *what's going on?*

One thing I knew, Sookie wouldn't be up to this on her own. She was being taught these things. I flashed back to the farm and remembered how Sookie would stare out at the lake all the time and seem so distant. What exactly was going on when I wasn't there?

Then it occurred to me. Sookie always seemed relieved to hang out with my teachers when she got here, as if she was trying to break away from my aunt's influence, so I was relieved when Ms. Grimmaar dismissed school early. She left with Ms. Dreeble and Sookie to go into town and keep her occupied until our aunt showed up. This would buy me some time to find out as much as I could before I questioned my sister.

Mr. Morrows rubbed his forehead and told us his head was splitting, and he went to his hotel room to sleep. The rest of the exchange students scattered, eager to clear away from the school before they caught the pox. That left Jasper, Clive, and me standing outside the school.

"I'll talk to Sookie later," I said quietly to Jasper. Clive didn't need to be in on everything, such as my sister having a stake in his witchcraft suspicions. "Right now, we've got to find out more about witchcraft in this town."

Clive, in his typical arrogant fashion, began taking charge. "Not every answer is in books, you know," he said to Jasper. "We should just go into town and start interviewing people. We should—"

I held up my hand to shut him down. As the other students inside the school began flooding out of their classrooms, I realized this was our opportunity to find some answers.

Seizing the chaotic moment, I said to Jasper and Clive, "Let's get inside the school before they lock up. There are no students or teachers, and I want to check out the classroom where we were working. Ms. Dreeble was sitting at the teacher's desk, and she always keeps a daybook."

What Clive had said about our teachers acting strangely was niggling at me. This wasn't the first time I'd seen adults fall under a spell. We plowed against the flow of students rushing to leave school, and it was as if I was a forward trying to make a break with the ball. Just like in soccer, I had to keep my elbows out to discourage jostling. Clive and Jasper followed behind.

Inside the school the halls were eerily quiet. Our feet tramped along and we jumped at our own echoing footsteps. Just as I suspected, Ms. Dreeble had left her daybook on her desk like she always did at Darkmont. It's just not polite to go through other people's things, but this was an emergency. As I opened the book and flipped through the pages, air escaped my lips in a hiss.

"This is so not good." I shoved the book across the desk for Jasper and Clive to see.

In the pages of Ms. Dreeble's daybook were her lesson plans for the whole school exchange. There was nothing written down on the persecution of witches. Instead, she'd planned lessons on important Swedish scientists and scientific discoveries. For the first day of class she'd planned a field trip to the house of a Nobel Prize–winning chemist. That field trip—and a dozen others—had never happened.

"We need to check if Mr. Morrows or Ms. Grimmaar left their daybooks behind." I shook my head. "Something's not right with them. I think they're under a glamour spell."

Jasper gulped and pulled out his feather from his belt. He waved it over the daybook and the white feather slowly turned green. "You're right. There is some kind of magic going on, so Ms. Dreeble is not seeing her original lesson plans."

Clive's eyes widened. "Can I take a look at that feather? What's it doing? How come you two seem to always know what's going on?"

There wasn't time to get into that now. I also didn't want Clive touching the feathers in case he remembered the last few fairy incidents. He didn't need to be reminded of Sookie's history with magic and of causing disaster, not when Clive's little brother was her best friend. I still wasn't sure how much I could trust him. To sidetrack him I said, "We better check the other classrooms before someone comes back."

The doors to the other rooms and the headmistress's office were locked. Jasper pointed down the hall. "Sometimes the keys are in a wall box in the head office."

"What are you kids doing here?"

We jumped and turned. A custodian came up and glared angrily at us. "The school's closed," he rasped. "Get out."

He didn't have to tell us twice. We fled.

"Now what?" I asked, rubbing my forehead. No library, no internet, no clues . . . this wasn't going well. I couldn't shake the feeling that something horrible was going on.

"Let's go back to my original plan," said Clive. "We'll go into the town and start asking people about the fog and why everyone seems so on edge."

Just ask people? That's not how it worked on television, which probably meant it was a good plan.

"Clive's right," I said, though those words didn't come easy. "Whatever it takes, we need to find out what this town is hiding."

CHAPTER 20

WALPURGIS NIGHT

Like a ghost town, Blakulla's sidewalks were deserted and many shops had closed by midday. Jasper, Clive, and I walked the few short blocks to the hotel where the Darkmont students were staying. There we split up, agreeing to meet back in the hotel lobby after an hour. We'd find out what we could about the weird fog and what seemed like a veil of secrecy around here. But we didn't have much time. My aunt would be at the school soon to pick up Sookie and me.

I struck out for the local shops as Clive lingered at the hotel talking to staff and Jasper checked the town library. Jasper said if he couldn't read in Swedish, he could at least talk to a librarian. Old habits die hard.

Many of the shop windows had new cards taped onto the glass, all with the same curious design. It was like a cross, but with what looked like the letter "H" drawn on each end. A coffee shop was still open, so I opened the door and stepped inside. The smell of dark roast coffee tantalized me; I knew Mom wouldn't approve of that. The door slammed shut and a bell jangled. The shopkeeper jumped in fright. Sorry I'd startled her, I began a conversation with the smattering of Swedish I'd learned.

"*Hej*," I said. "*Jag skulle vilja* ask a question, *snälla*. I've noticed a lot of shop windows have put a card in the door like yours. What is it for?" *Might as well get to the point,* I thought.

The tall, blond-haired woman drew a sign in the air and she didn't need to tell me it was for warding off evil. I'd seen enough late night black-and-white movies (the only horror shows Mom allowed me to watch) to know that's what people did before witches, werewolves, and vampires stormed the village.

She must have seen the worried look on my face because she laughed and said, "Don't worry, the signs are just an old tradition we follow for *Valborgsmassoafton*."

The shopkeeper stared at my puzzled face for a moment and then said, "We call it 'Walpurgis Night' in English. Tomorrow night is a big holiday for students. They make their way down to the lakeshore, build a big bonfire on the beach, and sing songs of spring. Do you do that at home?"

I shook my head, but it sounded fun.

"Sometimes children get sweets from neighbours. I think you do have a similar holiday." The woman stopped a second to think. "Yes, in October. I believe you call it 'Halloween.'"

Right. Just my luck to be in Sweden during the one week of the year that is like Halloween.

"Thank you, I mean, *tack*," and I flew from the store. I stood outside in the cold shadows of the lane until I caught my breath. Halloween was a time when the veil between our world and the fairy world lifted, allowing horrible things to happen. Why did I think that Grim Hill was the only place where that kind of trouble lurked?

I hurried back to the hotel where the three of us were joining up. Even though the shopkeeper seemed cheerful, I didn't believe she was telling me everything. She'd been startled when I first walked into her shop. And ancient tradition or not, when I'd asked about that sign, a shadow had crossed her face.

Before I stepped inside the hotel lobby, Clive whisked me from the door and hauled me out onto the promenade by the lake. A cold bitter wind cut through my jacket, even though the sun was shining again. He said, "Everyone is waiting for Walpurgis Night, and this year especially is unlike others in the past."

My eyes skimmed across the lake, and I could see another sickly fog boiling off the water and drifting to shore, patches of it shredding and hanging off the trees like cobwebs. I shuddered. Somehow I didn't think that fog was usually in the equation.

"The woman I talked to said the holiday was fun for kids." As the words left my mouth, it hit me: Halloween was supposed to be fun, too. It was all about dressing up and getting candy. I found out the hard way it also meant that diabolical forces could break through from the fairy world to ours at that time of the year.

Then Jasper rushed down the street and hurried onto the promenade. For a few moments, he gasped for breath. "Walpurgis," he sputtered. "It's a Celtic holiday."

"But this is Sweden!" I squeaked in fright. The Celts knew which times of year to prepare for otherworldly trouble. Clive looked from Jasper to me in confusion. For the moment we ignored him.

"The Celts migrated to many parts of Europe, *even* Scandinavia," Jasper said matter-of-factly. "Their traditions are widespread. But that's not all. This Celtic holiday is known for witches gathering and initiating new witches."

"That's what an old man told me in the hotel," Clive jumped in. "He told me his family always said when the fogs are out on Walpurgis Night, people should stay in because the witches come out." Then Clive added, "But a lot of young people around him laughed and said that was old superstition."

"I remember you telling me that witches and fairies are linked," I reminded Jasper.

Jasper nodded. "Witches gain power from fairy magic. They also use glamour and can trick people. They can use the magic to cast spells and," Jasper frowned with concern, "I found out something else . . . something you're not going to like."

"What?" My heart sped up.

"Witch trouble has been in this town for a long time, and while people don't really believe in it anymore, Blakulla, the mountain across the river, was supposed to be a place where witches met on Walpurgis. Those witches practised maleficium."

"Mal-what?" I asked.

"Maleficium is a powerful kind of magic used for evil." Jasper swallowed and adjusted the invisible glasses on his head, which he only did when he was in deep concentration. "The librarian translated different letters and journals dating back years. People in this town were horrible to witches, and for a long time they feared a terrible revenge. Some people believe that if the fogs ever occurred near Walpurgis Night, it was a sign that the witches were meeting to plot an evil revenge."

"That's not all," Clive said nervously. "After some people laughed at the old man who told me about Walpurgis, a few other people came up to him and asked if he'd seen the other signs. He nodded, and after they left I asked him what they had meant."

"Did he tell you?" I no longer needed the wind from the lake to chill my bones. A dread seeped into me as the fog crept closer to the shore like a hulking prehistoric beast closing in on the kill.

"No," said Clive. "That's when I saw you, but he's still inside waiting for me."

Clive, Jasper, and I rushed through the lobby. The old man was sitting alone at a table in the hotel café, sipping coffee and staring outside at the lake. The man set down his cup onto a dark walnut table and did that thing Jasper used to do. First he pushed his black glasses up on his nose, then he slipped them over his white, neatly combed hair and scrunched his eyes in concentration.

"May we join you, *snälla*?" I asked.

The old man smiled and gestured for us to sit down.

"Sir, you were going to tell me something about the strange signs happening in Blakulla?" Clive asked.

For a moment the man paused, as if he was weighing a decision. Then he said, "There are those that would think it best for me to keep my mouth shut. Mostly because they don't believe what I'm about to tell you. And I don't want to alarm children, but . . ."

The man fastened us with a serious stare. "There have been signs the witches are returning to this town. And that won't be good news for any young person."

"What do you mean?" I asked. But the man began gazing out the window again. The fog was almost here, and I shuddered to think it might bring those frogs and toads with it.

"Witches have always had it in for the children in this town," said the man.

"Specifically what kind of signs have you noticed?" asked Jasper.

"Four farmers have cows that are mysteriously sick. Not to mention, when they've been fetching their milk pails at the end of the day, all the milk has curdled."

I thought about the spooky reindeer herder on my aunt's farm at the mention of the milk pail, then I forced myself to focus on what the man was telling us.

"Also," said the man, "three boats have overturned in sudden winds on the lake and men have almost drowned."

"Those all have logical explanations," Clive ventured.

"Maybe," said the man. "But you don't live here. You haven't grown up with the stories, or even seen it happen before. Once, many years back when I was a boy, cows began falling ill and men did drown on the lake. Strange lights danced above old Blakulla, and as much as people wanted to believe it was the northern lights, I remember it differently."

"How?" I asked nervously.

The man stared at me. Then he reached into his pocket and pulled out a melted stub of black candle. "Because I was one of the children who didn't disappear."

CHAPTER 21

THE DISAPPEARED

A pall of subtle terror slipped over me in the hotel café. The way the old man clutched that piece of candle was the way I hung onto my feather when I needed to remember.

"Please," I said in a hushed voice, "tell us more."

The man winced as if something hurt badly, but then he shook it off. "When I was a boy I had a best friend. Lars and I were thick as thieves, running around this town, and I'll admit that sometimes we'd be up to no good," he smiled ruefully. "We had been looking forward to Walpurgis Night—had been planning mischief in fact. While people were attending the bonfires and not watching the rental shop, we were going to steal a boat for the evening and row across the channel to the mountain. But . . . but Lars never made it home that night. He never made it home again. And what I saw . . ."

The man trailed off, and no amount of polite prodding could get him to budge. Something tragic and terrifying had happened; I could tell by his haunted face. We sat quietly while he finished his coffee. Again he gave us a searching look. "I haven't seen this particular fog since that night when I learned the hard way how to look out for witches. By the kind of questions you are asking me," he favoured us with a serious stare, "perhaps it's best you learn those signs as well."

Jasper and Clive scraped their chairs closer to hear every word. I leaned over so far I almost fell off my chair.

"Witches are usually left-handed," the man said in almost a whisper. "They talk to themselves and, more importantly, they sing eerie songs to themselves." He went on. "They have light-coloured eyes and a familiar."

"What's a familiar?" I asked, hoping I didn't sidetrack him.

"A familiar is an animal that always hangs around the witch," he explained. "Witches use herbs and potions, and they have the ability to harm others."

I hung my head and it began to pound. I thought about that stupid black cat on the farm, and how it hung around my sister and always hissed at me. Sookie was left-handed and fair eyed; she also used herbs and potions. And since she learned how to talk, my sister had been muttering and singing to herself. I could feel the heat of someone staring at me and I looked up.

Jasper had gone pale and he'd fastened me with a worried gaze. I gave him a slight nod.

But Clive and the man hadn't noticed. Instead, the man kept talking. "Witches can change shapes," he added.

"Turn themselves into animals, or make themselves look less evil."

Sookie could do a lot of things, but she always looked like Sookie. Was she a witch or not? "Are people born witches?" I asked in confusion. "Jasper says that Walpurgis Night is a time to initiate witches."

The man nodded. "Your friend is correct. To become a full-fledged witch, you must go through a ritual on Walpurgis Night. Once you do, *there's no going back*."

Then a group of people entered the café and moved toward our table. The man was being joined by friends. We got up to give them our seats but as we started walking away, he quickly said, "One final sign is that witches use trolls to do their dirty work."

I guess Clive had gone as far with this as he could because he snorted and sputtered, "There's no such thing as trolls."

Another man who took a seat at our table and had no idea of our previous conversation laughed and said, "No one from these parts would agree with that. Everyone in Scandinavia believes in trolls." His eyes twinkled with amusement, but an uneasiness began gnawing at me as we walked back to the school.

Sookie wasn't the only one I knew who was left-handed or fair eyed or who talked to herself.

I stood in the parking lot shivering in the chill damp air as the fog settled in a thick ghostly blanket over Blakulla. Clive and Jasper braved the fog with me, as it seemed every other townsperson had hidden themselves inside their homes. Not even our friends left the hotel.

Clive rubbed his head vigorously. "My head is aching," he complained. "If nothing else, this mist isn't healthy." But the way Clive said it convinced me he knew there was something else.

Ms. Dreeble, Ms. Grimmaar, and Sookie returned to the school just as my aunt's truck turned into the parking lot.

"I'm staying home from school tomorrow," I told Jasper and Clive while the others were still out of earshot.

"Why?" Clive looked at me suspiciously.

"What is it, Cat?" Jasper's face brimmed with concern.

After talking to the man in the café, I couldn't hold back my suspicions any longer. Not with the troll connection and how glamour can make someone look different.

"Because," I said flatly, "I think my aunt might be a witch."

CHAPTER 22

THE FAMILY SECRET

That night I tossed and turned, and for the first time in a while, I had that dream again.

I'm running in the woods and it's as if the trees will lurch out and sweep me into their blackness where I'll be lost forever. Water rushes beneath my feet, and above me clouds fly across the sky faster and faster. I get dizzy looking at them, and I feel like my head's spinning. But it's me that's spinning and I'm tumbling to my death!

I woke up in a sweat and kicked off my quilt only to shiver in the freezing air.

"My stomach hurts," I said at breakfast, pushing my food away.

My aunt gazed at me for a moment and then said, "Well, best you go back to bed and rest." Then she pulled on her huge boots, wrapped a heavy scarf around her neck, and pulled a wool hat on her head. "It's time to feed the animals," she said briskly.

Sookie backed her chair away from the table, scraping it across the floor, and got her own things on. Pulling on her hat, she headed toward the door, eager to feed the chickens.

Before she left she turned to me. "Cat, do you know what I saw yesterday when I was with the teachers?" Her eyes blinked rapidly, and she looked upset.

"What?"

Sookie's eyes teared up. "We walked past a store and it had a sign saying reindeer meat was on sale. Oh, Cat," she sniffed, "do people eat reindeer?"

"Maybe the sign meant meat for the reindeer to eat," I lied.

"But reindeers are herbivores—they don't eat meat," Sookie said, unconvinced.

"Well, maybe it's not actual meat," I thought fast. "You know, like nuts are called meat."

"Maybe," Sookie said hopefully and she left.

No point telling her what those meatballs she gulped down were made of. Let her eventually figure out where ingredients came from when she was older. *In some ways, she acted like a normal little girl,* I tried to convince myself.

I grabbed a tart green apple from the fruit bowl because I was actually starving, and went to get my own clothes on so I could follow my sister and find out exactly how my aunt was preparing her to become a witch.

I hung in the shadows of the barn as Sookie scattered seed on the ground for the clucking chickens. Then she raced to the pasture and climbed over the fence, which my aunt had told her was *forbjuden*. She fed handfuls of hay to her favourite reindeer, the one she thought was Rudolph. Then Sookie headed for the lake.

For a moment I couldn't spot her among the tall reeds of lake grass. Then I heard the soft chilling song. My sister was singing an eerie tune and she was accompanied by an odd percussion. I crept closer.

Past the grass, waves lapped the rocky shore. Sookie sat on a log and sang a peculiar tune in a language I'd never heard. The black cat purred loudly, matching the song beat for beat.

As my sister sang, mystical fog steamed up from the edge of the lake and twisted its way toward the town. There was no doubt Sookie was causing it.

"Your sister possesses powerful magic," my aunt whispered behind me. "She would make a dangerous witch."

I jumped, and it was all I could do not to shriek. I turned my head and sputtered, "She is not a witch."

"Not yet," my aunt said quietly. "But I've tried all my influence to convince your sister not to use her magic. I've even taken her to your school every afternoon so that she'd stay away from that cat. But in the end, it must be your sister's choice.

"Listen to them now," my aunt's voice was full of sorrow. "That cat is teaching your sister a song of dark magic."

I shook my head in confusion. I thought my aunt was the witch. She had that creepy reindeer herder that sort of looked like a troll. She was with Sookie every morning, and my sister had to be learning magic from someone.

Was Aunt Hildegaard expecting me to believe a cat was teaching Sookie these things?

"So why wouldn't you just shoo away the cat?" I asked suspiciously. I stood up from my crouched position. But my aunt grabbed my hand in her calloused palm and tugged me behind a pine tree.

"Don't interrupt! It could be unsafe for your sister; she's in a trance. It would certainly be perilous for you. That evil creature will scratch out your eyes before your sister knows what's happening."

Still suspicious, I said, "So are you trying to tell me you're not a witch?"

"No, and neither are you," said my aunt.

I looked up at Aunt Hildegaard in surprise.

"When I met you girls for the first time, I wasn't prepared," Aunt Hildegaard said. *Not prepared for what?* I wondered.

"I needed to see, like I had with your mother, if you'd inherited the family legacy." My blood began to race. *Legacy?* My aunt continued in a harsh, whispery tone.

"I didn't think you were part of our family secret because your mother knew nothing about the shadowy world of magic." My aunt squeezed my hand slightly. "So it shocked me when I first greeted you both and sensed magic that poured from the two of you."

"But I don't have any magic ability," I squeaked in surprise.

"Perhaps not," my aunt mused, "but magic clings to you." Then she reached over and lifted a strand of my green hair.

"I realized when I met you both that I was in the presence of a powerful witch. Because of Sookie's tender age, I suspected you at first."

"Me?" I shook my head. "It's the fairies' fault you detect magic on me. I brushed up against a fairy lord once."

My aunt's eyes widened in surprise. "You've been in contact with the fairy world?"

"I carry this feather that I took from the fairies." I pulled out my white feather that was attached to my silver chain. "That's the magic you sense on me. I gave Sookie a feather, but she stopped wearing it." I frowned thinking about how my sister had been nothing but trouble since she had spent a short time in Fairy.

My aunt took my feather in her hand and closed her eyes. Then she looked at me. "You've taken something from the fairies," she said incredulously. "That is a courageous act."

I'd never thought of it that way, since I'd been scared to death the whole time. Behind us a hush stole over the forest that was deeply shadowed by rock cliffs and fir trees. The scent of pine and loamy, damp ground filled the air. But through the eerie quiet, my sister kept chanting in the distance.

"Why did you assume one of us was a witch? How do you feel magic?" I asked.

"I am a tenth generation witch fighter," said Aunt Hildegaard. "Back when the witch scares first overtook this medieval town, your ancestors fought against the witches."

"You mean our ancestors accused women of witchcraft?" I said startled and with more than a little guilt. Headmistress Grimmaar had said the townspeople had been especially cruel and heartless.

Aunt Hildegaard shook her head. "No one in our family was ever the accuser. But once a witch was spotted, we helped to drive them out. Not by murdering them," she shook her head sadly, "but by thwarting their magic—sabotaging their rituals, fighting against their spells. It was enough to drive them away."

I thought I understood. It was like how my friends and I fought magic by finding out our opponent's weakness.

"The medieval courts were the ones that murdered witches," my aunt said.

"Who were their accusers then?"

"Children," said my aunt. "Little children have a closer connection to the otherworld than adults. They could sense the women who had used fairy magic for evil."

For a while we stood there in the green silence of the forest. Then my aunt said, "I'm surprised that you can still detect fairy magic at your age. The older you become, the less magic feels real. If I wasn't cursed to keep the family secret going—to be the possessor of a witch's bell and to guard against dark magic—I would forget myself."

I pointed to my feather again. "This helps me remember."

"Of course," my aunt said. Was that admiration in her voice?

Then my aunt's words hit me. "Wait, what family secret?"

"After banishing witches for centuries, our family was placed under a powerful curse. Magic will always run through our family line. For every generation, a choice must be made to fight against magic or become its slave."

"But Mom isn't affected," I said hopefully, even though I knew she suffered from the magic without remembering.

"But you do have relatives that disappeared and have been forgotten," my aunt said. A cold chill crept into my heart. Sookie had already disappeared once and was forgotten until I fetched her back from Fairy.

My aunt, her voice brimming with sorrow, continued. "Back when I was a bit younger than you, a coven of witches had gathered on Walpurgis Night to bring revenge on the children who had betrayed them. My friends and I had discovered an old funicular that rode to the top of Blakulla Mountain. It has since been out of order; even then it was a rickety lift. Once we reached the top of the mountain, we crept up on their bonfire and managed to stop their ceremony. I grabbed the bell they used for their enchantment, and my friend grabbed their candle and extinguished the flame."

Then Aunt Hildegaard's voice broke. "But Lars had already disappeared by the time we arrived, and my own sister had already drunk from their cup and signed their book. She had already become a witch. I never saw her again after that night."

"How come my mom doesn't know anything about this?" I asked.

"Your own grandmother, my other sister, had already moved to North America when your mother was born. Even then she had no recollection of your other aunt. Like everyone else in this town, she too had forgotten her sister, one of the disappeared."

I remembered what the old man in the café had said about his friend never coming back, about children disappearing. He must have been with Aunt Hildegaard that Walpurgis Night.

"I'm not going to just wait for my sister to vanish," I said stubbornly.

"Of course not," said my aunt. "We have to fight for her."

At the thought of Sookie, I glanced back to the lakeshore. But Sookie had moved closer to the edge of the forest, and I could hear her talking to someone. In the shadows of the tree, I saw Sookie talking to the cat . . . and the cat was talking back!

My aunt and I ran toward my sister.

Then we froze in shock when the cat arched its back and was cocooned by a sickly, mustard-coloured smoke. The smoke roiled and grew, morphing into the shape of a person. Then like a mummy breaking out of its sarcophagus, Ms. Grimmaar stepped from the smoke. The cat, our headmistress, was a shape-shifting witch!

"Now we must prepare for your initiation," Ms. Grimmaar said to Sookie.

"I've made a terrible mistake." My aunt's forlorn voice

echoed doom. "I've led your sister right into the arms of the witch."

She wasn't the only one. My stomach sickened when I thought of how relieved I was that Sookie had been hanging around with my teachers instead of staying at the farm in the afternoons. All along, while we had morning class with Ms. Dreeble and Mr. Morrows, Ms. Grimmaar had been tutoring Sookie in casting dark spells.

"Sookie," I shouted. Finally, I was able to move and sprang forward.

Sookie turned once and glanced back at me. Then she ran off with Ms. Grimmaar into the waiting darkness of the woods.

CHAPTER 23

THE BRIDGE

I raced into the dark, forbidding forest after Sookie.

My aunt shouted behind me, "Come back! You do not want to get lost in the forest on Walpurgis Night." But I kept on running.

Then in a resigned voice, Aunt Hildegaard called after me, "Do not let Sookie drink from the cup or sign the book. If she does, she'll be lost forever."

I ran faster. But the gloom of the forest blackened the path, and the trees twisted in every direction, creating a hopeless maze. I stopped for a second, held my breath, and listened. Several yards away I heard the crunch of pine needles.

Mustering the stealth I used to sneak up on an opposing soccer player, I crept up on them. Ms. Grimmaar had seemed like such a cool teacher, and even now she seemed so beautiful with her dark hair and piercing light eyes. Then I remembered the words from the town statue: *Fair is foul.* They had that right.

Just as I lurched out of the trees to make a grab for my sister, a cruel cackle in the distance set my teeth on edge.

It was a trap.

A small black bear rooted around in the clearing, and I carefully backed away into the trees. My heart pounded in my throat, but the bear ignored me as I turned and ran, leaping through bushes and jumping over thick roots and fallen branches.

The forest came alive with screeches, clomps, and squeals while animals joined in a chorus. Still I searched for my sister, but it was as if the trees shifted every time I turned, and I found myself back at the clearing with the bear. Once more I backed away, although this time the bear glanced my way and growled menacingly. I had to get a grip and pay better attention. I didn't think the bear would ignore me a third time.

Through the winding path and dense clumps of trees, I kept moving. Sometimes I heard my sister's shrill laughter and Ms. Grimmaar's cackle, but they were getting farther away. Above me clouds moved in and covered the sky as the air thickened with a coming storm. Soon icy sleet began to fall.

I looked at the sky and decided to follow the direction of the clouds, which began streaming faster and faster across the horizon. If nothing else, following their direction would keep me from running in circles and stumbling back on that bear.

The wind picked up and began to screech in my ears, and I felt the temperature drop. My ears ached and I covered them with my hands. As if from nowhere, dark clouds blackened the sky and a muffled roar broke from above. Hailstones thundered down, bending and snapping branches, and I dived under the sweeping arms of a huge fir tree. The hailstones were as large as my thumb and they bounced high off the forest floor.

Hugging the tree trunk, I wanted to give up. It was impossible to get anywhere in this shifting, uncanny forest, and I couldn't stop shivering. *Courage, Cat*, a small voice inside me whispered. The voice would have to do a lot better than that. Then I heard Sookie close by.

"Are we going to see Santa?" She sounded excited.

"Soon," said Ms. Grimmaar.

My blood began to boil at the way the witch was manipulating my sister. Anger flooded through me, and I warmed up, so that when the hail stopped moments later, I was back on the trail and closing in.

I'd finally caught sight of Sookie and Ms. Grimmaar as they crossed a bridge over a violently churning river. They had disappeared into the forest on the other side, and I began crossing the rickety wood and rope suspension bridge. It was the sound of the water as it churned beneath me that triggered my memory. But I was already halfway across the bridge when I remembered my dream—

Then I froze.

A feeling of déjà vu overwhelmed me—those flashes of memory that told me I had been here before, even if it was impossible. The water boiled furiously below the bridge, the dark clouds scudded across the sky above me, and in the distance I heard the witch cackle. I'd definitely done this before, even if it was in a dream. Beneath me the bridge began to sway, and I got that stomach sickening feeling from my nightmare. But this time I was wide awake.

I'm going to die, I thought. *This is where I drown*. In that split second I'd remembered my encounter with the Sámi shaman back at the amusement park in Stockholm and how she told me I would drown. My knees buckled.

"Cat," a voice shouted, "watch out!"

But it was too late. A three-fingered hand grabbed the suspension rope and with amazing power gave it a treacherous twist. The bridge dipped and slipped from under my feet, and I was pitched head first into the icy water.

Down I went as the freezing water made it impossible for me to move my arms and legs. *It's just like my dream*, I thought calmly. The cold felt like I had dived into a tub of ice cubes. It was no surprise when I felt a tug on my leg. But when I looked below, it wasn't the Sámi shaman.

It was something far more hideous.

I screamed, but only a stream of bubbles escaped my mouth. The last thing I remember was hearing the deep, muffled echo of something else plunging into the water.

Then I sank into utter darkness.

CHAPTER 24

GNAWER OF THE MOON

"Wake up!" the gravelly voice shot into my ear, making it ache.

I tried to take a breath but only choked as an icy, disgusting swill of water sloshed in my lungs. A gush of ice and fire burned down my throat and into my chest, then another and another until I was retching up slimy bilge that had a lingering taste of fish.

Sputtering and coughing, I finally opened my eyes and tried to make out the hulking shadows in the gloom. I was inside a damp, dripping cave that smelled like a garbage can and was lit by several smoking torches.

"You're alive," Clive said in relief. "I thought you were a goner."

My arms and legs wouldn't move as if they were anchored to heavy stones. I blinked and gasped as my heart caught in my throat. On the other side of the cave, what I thought were three big rocks moved. One was creeping toward me.

"We're kind of out of the fire into the frying pan," Clive said with a hint of despair.

The ugly creature I'd seen pulling me down to my watery death loomed before me. He reminded me slightly of my aunt's reindeer herder, that is, if the reindeer herder had a hideous monster for a cousin.

The beast hulking over me was covered in wiry mats of hair. His huge horn-like ears pointed sharply away from his head, and his eyes glowed a menacing orange. His flesh clung to him in corpse grey, and he reached toward me with three long sausage fingers ending in cruel black talons, the thumb curled into a horrible claw. I gulped. There was no doubt about it: we were surrounded by trolls.

An argument broke out among the three creatures, and they sounded like enormous cats fighting over fish bones, all snaps and hisses and feral growls.

"They're mine," complained the first troll who had been reaching for me. "I've been fishing for weeks, and so it's my catch. I was thinking of making them slaves, but I've been craving human flesh lately."

"I caught the boy," said another troll, "so back off."

"You have to share," complained the third, who was uglier than the other two, if possible. "I shared my dinner with you last month."

"Nasty bony fishes those were," spat the first troll. "And the old leather boot you pulled from the river bed was hardly a feast."

A cold chill settled over my already frozen spine. We'd been captured by the most dangerous trolls of all: water trolls.

"Crap," I muttered.

"No one is eating the girl," a voice spoke out of the shadows. "Gnawer of the Moon, even though you are my brother, I am also bound to this girl's aunt, whose farm I protect. The girl has fed me milk, and in return I have given her the breath of life."

Then from the shadows emerged my aunt's reindeer herder, Osgaard. I knew he was evil.

"I tried to give you mouth-to-mouth resuscitation," whispered Clive, "but you were turning blue until he breathed air into your lungs."

My first thought was, *Clive's lips touched mine*? Even though I was shivering with cold, my face began to burn. I tried to sort out the last events as they sluggishly unfolded in my mind. It was as if my brain had become waterlogged as well.

Ugh. No wonder my breath tasted gross; I had been resuscitated by a troll.

Then I remembered the rest of the words on the town statue: *foul is fair*. More gratefully, I muttered to Osgaard, "Thank you for saving me. But please don't eat my friend."

"I am not bound to the boy," Osgaard said, shaking his head sadly.

Gnawer of the Moon smiled in a nasty, twisted grimace. "I want to eat. I'll need my strength, for tonight I help the witches." He puffed his chest in pride, informing us, "I am keeper of the bell, book, and candle."

"You're helping *the witches?*" My thoughts began to race. That meant Gnawer of the Moon knew where the witches would meet. I had to stop that ceremony. I also had to stop the trolls from eating Clive.

"Um, Cat, how are you managing to talk to those creatures?" Clive had shimmied across the stone floor to get closer to me.

Thinking of what Osgaard had said, I asked Gnawer of the Moon, "So do you like milk?"

That got all the trolls' attention. "Milk is delicious," the other three said.

"Lovely milk," said Gnawer with longing. "But nasty farmers put salt around their barns, and we cannot cross. And we can't go out in daylight, so we never get sweet milk."

"Cat, what are they saying?" Clive's gaze bobbed frantically between me and the trolls.

I wasn't sure how I was talking to the trolls, but it didn't seem any different than talking with Clive. "I'm, um, negotiating." Clive didn't need to know the trolls had it in mind to eat him, at least not for the moment.

"I'll give you milk if you let us free," I offered. "I'll give you each a huge glass of milk." When they hesitated I said, "I'll give you two glasses of milk."

Gnawer stuck out a gruesome black tongue and licked his lips. Then he wavered when he said, "But I need my energy to help the witches tonight. I must hold the book for the new witch to sign and use troll magic to light the candle and ring the bell. Troll magic runs on meat." He looked again at Clive.

My heart sped up. "Why do you want to help the witches anyway?" I squeaked. Then more thoughtfully I added, "They don't speak kindly of you."

"What do you mean?" Gnawer snarled.

I gulped. Right, Cat, make the troll angry. Way to go. "Well, whenever Ms. Grimmaar—I mean, the head witch—talks about trolls, she calls you stupid."

The trolls howled and Clive asked in alarm, "What's going on?"

"Do you lie?" Gnawer bellowed.

"The child is a speaker of truth like her aunt," said Osgaard.

"What do you know?" another troll growled at him. "You've been protecting that woman's farm for so long, Night Roamer, you've even taken a human name. You are a tomtar now, not a troll. And," he spat in disgust, "you're beginning to look and smell human."

Osgaard didn't smell that human to me. Again I wiped my mouth.

"And I've been with humans long enough to know this child speaks the truth and it's the witches who lie."

The trolls grouped on the other side of the cave to make their decision. Again they hissed and growled while Clive and I moved closer to each other, shivering in our soggy, freezing clothes.

"I came to the farm to check on you," whispered Clive. "Your aunt told me you'd gone after your sister and she was worried. We split up to search for you and, well, when I saw you fall into the river . . ."

"You jumped in after me," I finished. Clive was insanely brave.

Now we were the trolls' prisoners, and time was running out. We huddled miserably, and when our teeth began chattering, Osgaard threw a stinking fur hide over us. We accepted it with gratitude.

The trolls debated for a long time; they didn't seem to be fast movers. Osgaard kept coming over and giving us updates.

"There's still the problem of the witches," Osgaard shook his head, giving Clive a mournful look. "They control trolls, and they can be most cruel. My brother and cousin are wondering if they should just eat the boy and obey the witches."

Because Osgaard spoke to us in halting English, Clive let out a yelp. "Couldn't they just pretend to help the witches?" he said quickly. "Aren't trolls clever enough to trick the witches?"

That got Gnawer's attention, and I realized his pride had been hurt when I told him the witches called trolls stupid. So I added, "The witch also said you were nasty, lazy, filthy creatures." I looked around the cave that was littered with fish bones, old junk tires, and bottles, and strangely, I caught an occasional glimpse of silver. "Um . . .

no offence. If you let us go," I bargained, "we will help you defeat them and you'll be free of their control."

"Then we will help you trick them," decided Gnawer. "How?"

"I've got an idea," I said. Clive had been onto something. We could fake a move, like in soccer when you aim the ball one way and then deke it back for another player to make a breakaway.

I remembered back to the hotel room in Stockholm when Sookie had stayed up all night practising her signature. Even then Ms. Grimmaar had been preparing Sookie for the Walpurgis ceremony.

"Yes, I have a plan."

CHAPTER 25

THE WITCHES' REVENGE

By the time the trolls released us, the sun had sunk on the horizon. A stab of fear sliced my heart: Walpurgis Night was hastening upon us. In the twilight shadows of the forest, Gnawer of the Moon, Osgaard, and their two cousins followed us back to the farm. We took a gloomy winding path so they could stay safely in the shadows and out of the dying sun. Weird, even in twilight I could clearly see the highest leaf on the tallest tree, not to mention hear the tiniest crack of a branch above me.

"Good heavens," said Aunt Hildegaard when Clive and I walked to the cabin with the trolls in tow.

Quickly, I explained to my aunt the bargain I had struck with the trolls. While she stood on the porch and ladled milk out of her jug and into their gaping maws, Clive and I went into the house to prepare. I loaned Clive a thick flannel shirt that my aunt kept hanging on a hook in the kitchen and a warm wool hat. I put on my warmest jacket and threw stick matches into my pocket. There was no time to change out of my jeans, which had dried and were now stiff and itchy.

Going into our bedroom, I grabbed a sheet of paper from Sookie's notebook, tape, and a fat glue stick. When we returned to the kitchen, Clive grabbed the box of salt sitting on the counter. "If salt keeps trolls from crossing, maybe it will—"

"—work on other supernatural creatures, like witches," I finished for Clive. "Good idea; I'm sure it will."

Both Clive and I were half-starved, so we also grabbed bananas and a slice each of the dark brown bread. We stuffed our faces as we rushed outside, where we found the trolls arguing, again. They hissed like a nest of snakes, and Gnawer was complaining that my aunt had short-changed them.

"We only got one glass of milk when we were promised two."

"You'll get the second glass of milk once you've fulfilled the last part of the bargain," I said. "And as a bonus, you can each have a ladle of cream."

The trolls crowed in delight and my aunt gave me a surprised look. "You speak troll?" she said. "And how did you know I was already going to offer them cream?"

"Yeah, you seem to know what I'm going to say before I say it," added Clive.

Osgaard leaned over and whispered into my aunt's ear. When he had finished explaining, she regarded me with a curious stare. "You are indeed a strong child. Not many could endure the breath of a troll. Pure magic has filled your lungs."

So that's why my chest kept tingling and there was an odd buzzing in my ears—not to mention the night vision.

"Hey," I said to Gnawer, "stop licking the glue stick. You need it for tonight."

Gnawer snarled, so I quickly added, "Then you can eat the whole thing if you want." He seemed satisfied with that. I took a belled reindeer collar off a hook in the barn, and Gnawer had everything he needed. I hoped Osgaard would go through the plan with him one more time.

The trolls lumbered away with Osgaard the Night Roamer, and Clive and I piled into my aunt's truck to set out for town. We were going to need reinforcements.

While my aunt waited in her truck, I had run to the hotel to find Jasper.

We were now standing across the channel from Blakulla, its hulking spike looming over us. Northern lights streaked the sky in ominous ghostly light that danced and twisted in glowing reds.

"Cat, you've got to see this," Jasper urged. He held a book in front of me, and my eyes widened in surprise.

The tooled leather and strange runes on the cover were a smaller version of a magic book I'd seen once before, in a place I didn't care to remember. Jasper was holding out a *grimoire*!

"I got the idea from you, Cat. When you took a look at Ms. Dreeble's book, and we realized she was under a spell, I started to wonder how the spell was affecting Ms. Grimmaar." Then he shook his head ruefully. "I thought all I had to do was check her daybook on the desk in her office like you did." Jasper's face burned red. "So I, um, snuck the keys from the cabinet in the office."

Then he continued. "Her office is one strange place, Cat, cluttered with jars of creepy-looking roots and slimy eyes of newts, and bottles of phosphorescent green and yellow liquids that seem to boil inside their stoppers. I walked past her bookshelf . . ." Jasper stopped to gulp.

"And?" Trepidation made me quiver, or was it Osgaard's troll breath still rattling around inside me?

"It was as if my feather was going to sear right through my skin. So I pulled the feather out and waved it over the shelf. It lit up brightest next to this book." Jasper began to flip the pages. "At first I couldn't read anything. It was all in runes."

"Now check this out." Jasper passed his feather over the page.

I gasped. The ink letters shimmied and shifted and then I read:

To become a witch, one must undergo the ritual of bell, book, and candle. First, the bell will be rung through the town, and it will lure the magically inclined. Burn the black candle of dark magic during the ceremony on Walpurgis Night. Once the new witch drinks from the cup and signs the book of witches, she will be forever bound.

Then added on the page in a spidery scrawl was a note. *The little girl has the strongest fairy magic I have ever encountered. She heard the summons of the bell from a distance. If you lure the child, we can channel her powers. When the students gather on the shore on Walpurgis Night for their celebrations, we will have the ability to drown them all. We will finally exact our revenge.*

"No," I said softly. The witches were going to use Sookie to drown the town's students. I had to stop my sister and the witches. But could I fight my family curse?

"The Sámi shaman knew," I said miserably. "I survived drowning, and now things are worse."

Jasper gave me a worried look and started to speak, but I cut him off.

"You're right," I sighed. "Now's not the time to worry about what's ahead. It's time for action."

"How did you know that's what I was going to say?" Puzzled, Jasper frowned.

"Long story," I said, which wasn't really the truth, but explaining that magical troll breath was helping me read minds seemed weird. Instead, I ran out of the hotel to tell my aunt the terrible news. She told me to wait for her here, and drove off to find townspeople to help.

But I worried we were already too late. Bonfires dotted the stretch of beach. The channel cut right to the lake, and I knew hundreds of students would be gathering there as well to sing and celebrate Walpurgis Night.

We couldn't wait. We gathered our friends, and like the times before, they didn't need a long explanation. It was as if their subconscious understood there was trouble. With the help of Mitch, who seemed to know a lot about breaking locks, we got into the boat rental booth and dragged out two rowboats.

Mitch, Mia, Amarjeet, and Amanda piled into the first boat. "Good thing I joined the rowing club last summer," Mia said, taking charge of her crew.

Zach took a handful of krona out of his pocket and counted it on the counter of the rental booth. Checking the sign on the wall, he said, "What do you think: three hours?" Then he laid the cash next to the till.

"Shouldn't you be in the other boat?" Clive suggested when Zach took a seat beside me, forcing Clive to sit beside Jasper.

"Shouldn't you?" Zach said cheerfully and pulled the oar.

As we swept out into the deep, freezing water, I hoped I wasn't leading my friends to their doom.

CHAPTER 26

BELL, BOOK, AND CANDLE

The rocky shores of Blakulla were cruel and forbidding. Black branches floating on the surrounding water made it difficult for us to make our way across. One of the rowboats scraped against a jagged rock, and we stepped into icy water up to our knees. Mitch and Amarjeet hauled the first boat to shore, while Clive and Zach hauled the other. Mia and Amanda secured the oars under the seats in each boat. Jasper and I followed along the rocky coast looking for the thin line that would mark the derelict funicular: our passageway up.

"There it is," Jasper pointed. "Are you sure it works?"

The path up the mountain was steep and treacherous; it would take hours to climb, hours we didn't have. "It is out of order, has been for years." I gulped. "But we've got no choice."

Eight of us jammed into the rusted funicular while Mitch fiddled with the electrical box outside. The metallic beast groaned and shook menacingly on its cable, and the bull wheels screamed in protest until we lurched forward. Mitch jumped inside. The funicular swung from side to side, and we rocked with it. Then it steadied and began a slow trek up the mountain as we stared at the distance below. If this thing fell off its cable, we'd be crushed.

Creaking and groaning, the funicular rattled up the mountain. I hoped that witches didn't have good hearing.

"Look, Cat," Jasper said in alarm.

From this height on Blakulla, I gazed below at the hundreds of bonfires along the shores of the lake and canal. It looked like Aunt Hildegaard wasn't having much success getting the students off the beaches. Our luck needed to change.

As we climbed higher, I explained the plan to rescue Sookie to my friends. No one questioned that we were on a witch hunt.

"Why does it feel as if we've done something like this before?" Amarjeet's face scrunched in concentration.

"Because we have," Mia said in a hollow voice. "More than once, I think."

Zach and Mitch nodded in agreement. *Was witch glamour as strong as fairy glamour?* I wondered. *Would they forget this like the other times?* A small, unwelcome voice piped up inside me, *That is, if we even survive.*

Finally, the funicular groaned to a stop, and we stepped out into the black forest. "There," I pointed to a yellow glow seeping through the trees. A large bonfire blazed a short distance away. We hurried, but as we neared the bonfire we hung back in the shadows behind a line of skeletal black trees. "Make sure no one doubles round and sneaks up on us from behind," I whispered to Mia, Amanda, and Mitch, while Clive gave them each pockets full of salt. Amarjeet and Zach covered the other side, while Jasper, Clive, and I crept forward.

The witches were gathered in a large circle, and the orange-yellow flames of their fire roared and danced. Sookie stood near the centre looking slightly ridiculous in her gigantic witch's hat. But I knew there was nothing ridiculous about it—my sister was a powerful magician, and if she unleashed those powers, I feared for us all. I crept a little closer to the light, and my mouth dropped in horror.

Through the blur of yellow flame, I made out several familiar faces. Leering at the fire was the kind woman at the troll shop back in Stockholm. I would never forget the contrast of her young face and grey hair. I would also never forget that it was the bell on her shop that had summoned Sookie.

Anne Britt and Helga stood a few feet away from me dressed in witches' cloaks and brimmed hats. So did several other students from our classes. But that wasn't what was chilling my bones.

Under the light of the moon, their yellow witch's eyes glowed with thin slits of black. The cat eyes stared cruelly at my sister, malice and evil twisting their faces into ugly masks. It was now clear that the horrific face I'd seen staring into our room that night had been Ms. Grimmaar.

No, Sookie, no! I held my breath when Gnawer of the Moon stepped out from behind a tree carrying a bell, a book, and a candle.

"Let the initiation begin." Ms. Grimmaar's voice rang out in icy tones that sent chills up my arms and neck.

The witches hoisted Sookie onto a litter draped in black silk that hung from the stretcher like a vampire's cape. They carried her to a huge tree trunk shrouded in a tablecloth of flimsy cobwebs. Gnawer stepped in front of her and placed a thick black wax candle in an old-fashioned candleholder on top of the cloth.

Mom would have said it was a total fire hazard.

Then Gnawer set the book at the bottom of the tree, and a small gasp escaped my lips. The luminous crescent moon, a witch's moon, decorated its cover and had begun to glow, pulsating like a beating heart. Finally, he set the large pewter bell beside the candle.

I hoped no one noticed when Gnawer turned his back from the wind to light the candle, so that he could really light the candle with stick matches instead of troll magic. He spun around as the candle spewed thick, sulfurous black smoke that stank and made my eyes water.

Chanting, the witches' voices pinched my nerves like chalk's jagged scrapes across a blackboard. Ms. Grimmaar walked over and flipped the book open. The other witches lowered the litter and set Sookie down. My little sister stumbled toward the book as if she was in a trance.

Ms. Grimmaar handed my sister a quill pen with a black feather plume and a nib dipped in crimson ink. "You must sign the book of witches. Use your best signature, because it will remain in this book for all time."

I held my breath as Sookie took the pen and with her tongue sticking out of the side of her mouth, laboured with her tidiest letters. No one noticed that the page she signed was from her own notebook that Gnawer had glued on top of the actual book page. When he turned away from the witches, he carefully slipped the fake page out before slamming the book shut.

"Our newest and most powerful witch has signed the book of our coven, and has dedicated herself to maleficium —dark magic." They began cackling and it grew louder.

Ms. Grimmaar lifted the bell and said in a voice that seemed to suck any warmth from the air, "Bell, book, and candle, we ring in the witch."

She shook it, and amidst all the cackling, no one noticed that the taped bell didn't ring. Instead Gnawer rang the reindeer collar that he hid behind his back.

Right, I thought, *if Sookie hasn't really signed the book, and the candle didn't light by troll magic, and the bell didn't ring, she's not a witch.*

Then it all went wrong.

Ms. Grimmaar stared suspiciously at the bell and then past the witch circle into the trees. Jasper, Clive, and I stepped back into the shadows. Suddenly Anne Britt swept open her cape and produced a pewter chalice that looked like a goblet the Vikings had used. Inside the goblet swirled a frothing, bubbling green witch's brew. I'd forgotten about the last part of the ritual, where the new witch drank from the cup.

"No!" I broke from the trees as Jasper and Clive tried to grab me back. "Sookie, don't drink it!"

CHAPTER 27

ESCAPE FROM BLAKULLA

I grabbed at the pewter cup to yank it from Sookie's hand, but before I could, a claw dug cruelly into my shoulder. Pain shrieked down my arm and back. Ms. Grimmaar wrenched my arms behind me and I couldn't move.

"Sookie, throw down the cup!" I cried.

But Sookie looked as though she was staring into a completely different place; her glazed eyes passed over me as if I wasn't there. She lifted the cup to her lips, opened her mouth, and began to drink the green brew.

I lifted my leg and aimed as if I was going to kick a soccer ball out of mid-air. My foot connected with the goblet, and it flew out of Sookie's hands. As it spun around in the sky, the frothing potion spilled out, phosphorescent droplets flying into the air. Where they landed the grass glowed in the dark.

A steel vise kept squeezing my shoulder until it brought me to my knees with a gasp. In a haze of agony, I could hear Clive and Jasper pushing and shoving their way to us. Suddenly, Ms. Grimmaar let out a shriek.

"Back away," she cried as if she was also in terrible pain. "This child wears silver, and it burns."

Ms. Grimmaar had leaned over to grasp my fairy feather and must have brushed against my silver belt. She held out her hand, which showed a horrible burn. Seizing the second of freedom, I jumped up and grabbed Sookie's arm.

"Come with us." I tried yanking my sister away, but it was as if she weighed a thousand pounds. Then I remembered what Aunt Hildegaard had said: Sookie had to choose. I couldn't force her to come with us; her magic was too strong.

Jasper and Clive leaped forward before the witches could surge in and they poured salt in a circle around us. This kept the angry witches at bay.

"Sookie, the witches are going to hurt a lot of people," I pleaded as they shrieked at us like a crazed chorus of maniacs.

"They're teaching them a lesson," Sookie said, and her voice drifted as if she were only half there. "The children were bad to witches before."

"Maybe," I said, "but they were doing what they were told. Besides, they have been gone for centuries, Sookie. The kids the witches want to hurt now haven't done anything to them."

"The town needs a lesson," Sookie said in that distant voice.

"So you really intend to drown them?" This didn't sound like something my sister was capable of.

"No . . . scare them," Sookie said brokenly, and for the first time I thought I saw a flash of consciousness when her eyes began blinking. "We're going to scare them by making waves get big in the channel. The waves will pour onto the shore and extinguish the bonfires. Then they'll all run away and their fun night will get wrecked."

"What if they don't get away in time?" I pleaded.

Sookie shook her head slowly. "I . . . I . . ."

"And think of the reindeer," I pointed out as my mind raced. "Aunt Hildegaard's reindeer pen is at the lakeshore. If a big wave comes, Rudolph will be trapped."

"No . . ." whispered Sookie as her face crumpled in dismay. My sister began backing away from the witches' circle. Ms. Grimmaar and the others shrieked in anger, and it was as if steel daggers sliced my heart.

"Hurry," I gasped.

We stretched out my silver chain between us, and Jasper and Clive walked along the middle, pouring a trail of salt from their pockets. We hurried to the funicular as the forest seemed to turn against us. Wind whipped up in a fierce frenzy, tearing branches from the trees. Brooms of evergreen flew everywhere, one smashing down and poking me near the eye.

"Ow!" A branch of pine smacked Clive in the head. Jasper ducked just in time as an uprooted birch tree dived down from the sky and stuck in the ground like a pitchfork.

"The witches are using the elements of earth, air, and fire against us," said Sookie as the ground began to shake. A flaming branch streaked across the sky and landed next to us on a tree, which burst into flame.

Our friends waited by the funicular. They'd made a clear path for us lined with salt, and we raced the last several feet. Mitch had already tampered with the battered electrical box and the grind of gears was in full hum. The four of us leaped inside the crowded gondola and Mitch swung back the lever, putting the funicular in full power as we raced down the mountain.

Faster and faster we hurtled down Blakulla's steep and treacherous slope. My stomach flipped as if I was careening along in a rollercoaster.

"Maybe you better hit the brakes," Amarjeet gasped as she clutched onto a leather strap. We were all holding on for our lives.

"I . . . can't," Mitch shouted as he pulled a side lever on the car. He kept yanking but the funicular didn't slow down.

CHAPTER 28
SÁMI MAGIC

The bottom of the mountain raced toward us. Would we fly off the cable and spin to our deaths, or would the car crash at the bottom of the mountain and crush us all?

The funicular plummeted. I clutched onto Sookie, and we all crouched on the floor to save ourselves from flying around. Then in rapid motion the funicular lurched forward, pulled back, lurched again, and stopped. For a second, darkness spun in front of my eyes as my head slammed against the side of the car.

"We . . . we've stopped," gasped Mia.

We were all lying in a pile at the bottom of the funicular. As I scrambled up I could see a three-fingered hand clutching the side of the cable car, and a long, hairy grey arm holding it back. Actually, a lot of arms were holding onto the funicular. I moved to the window. A dozen trolls had surged under the speeding car and raced along, jumping onto it, slowing it down, and then at the very last minute, dragging it to a stop. I promised myself to give the trolls every last drop of cream on the farm.

"We've got to hurry," Sookie urged. "I think we made the witches very mad."

The trolls fled back into the forest, so it seemed they were nothing but shadows and tricks of our imagination.

"What was that?" Amarjeet gasped.

The sky blazed brown and then sickly green as a skull white fog rolled down Blakulla's mountain slope. Its foul stench sickened our stomachs.

"Hurry," said Jasper. "Let's get to the boats."

We scrambled across the rocky shore and waded into ice water up to our knees. I hesitated for a second as uneasiness seeped into me. The thought of bobbing along a deep canal in a rickety rowboat made my heart hammer.

"What is it, Cat?" Sookie frowned, looking worried herself.

"Nothing," I said. Maybe I'd just had enough water for one day. I jumped into the rowboat and hauled Sookie in after me. We dug in our oars and began to row.

As we moved away from the shore, a strange whooshing grew into an earsplitting roar as the white fog twisted itself into a full-fledged tornado.

"Pull in your oars and hold on," screamed Mia as the tornado descended upon us.

The calm waters quickly turned into shooting white water rapids, and our boats rocked, bounced, and spun. I pushed Sookie into the bottom of our boat and lay on top of her as I clung to the sides. It was all we could do to keep ourselves from being tossed out into the boiling water. But we were all strong athletes, and we hung on even when the boats arced and stood straight up in the water before slamming back down and tipping us from side to side.

All of a sudden the fog lifted and the boats stopped dead in the water. Then it grew ominously quiet. "I don't like this," whispered Sookie, her eyes darting back and forth as she stared past the blackness to the distant shore.

"Watch out for the water, Cat," my sister said in an eerie voice. Once more a chilling sense of déjà vu swept over me.

"What?" Dread clutched my heart.

A creepy sucking sound echoed across the canal, and our boat dipped as if someone had pulled the plug and the water was swirling down the drain.

"Oh, my god." The softness in Amanda's voice made her words more chilling than a scream. We looked behind as an enormous tidal wave grew in the distance. As it roared closer, it collected height. In seconds, the wave was as tall as a five-storey building and heading straight toward us. So the witches had stolen enough of Sookie's magic to carry out their wicked plan. We were all going to drown.

"Turn the boats!" Mia shouted. "Steer into the wave."

We pulled frantically at the oars and turned our boats around as the towering wave swept us up. But we all knew we were doomed.

"We need to fight back with magic," Sookie shouted. She scrunched her face and began murmuring. But her song was hardly a hum. "I'm not strong enough," she moaned. "Too much of my magic is with Ms. Grimmaar. I have to get it back so I can reverse the water spell."

"How?" I shouted against the roaring wave.

"By making a stronger spell than hers," Sookie wailed.

We only had seconds.

They say when you are about to die your life flashes before your eyes. But the only flash I got was my last happy moment at Gröna Lund before the shaman had wrecked the night. She'd been right; first I'd drown, then worse would happen. My friends and sister would drown with me, and so would lots of innocent people.

Ugly cold fear began darkening my mind until a shard of hot anger broke through.

The shaman had said the fates were against me, but she'd also said to fight them. Only I could decide my own fate. And whatever happened, I was going down kicking. My mind spun as I tried to think of any way to fight against the witches.

The shaman said I had to use my magic. And she'd given me a knotted rope that she had said bound the elements of nature. Okay, my mind raced, those are earth, air, fire . . . and *water*. I dug into my jacket pocket and pulled the knotted rope. I still didn't see what magic—

Then I felt my skin tingle, like I was standing too close to a Halloween sparkler. Osgaard's magic! Troll magic still burned inside my lungs. "Hold on to us!" I shouted to Clive, Amanda, Jasper, and Zach. They anchored us with their arms and legs as I grabbed Sookie's hands in mine.

It was as if lightning shot through us. I swear my hair stood on end. Sookie began singing one of her creepy songs, and this time her voice carried over the storm and the roar of the tidal wave. Still the wave grew, and our rowboat lifted higher, about to be tossed down like a little toy falling from a giant's hand.

I clutched the cord the shaman had thrust in my hand. *Use this against the forces of nature.* What I had to do suddenly made sense. "We have to untie the knots of nature," I yelled to Sookie. "That will undo the spells the witches have cast."

With one hand still clasped in Sookie's, I untied a knot in the rope with my free hand. The roar damped as the wind died down. We untied another knot. The wave didn't crest; instead, the water began streaming in the other direction when the earth shook beneath the water. We untied a third knot, and the wave flattened, setting both the rowboats on the churning water that circled like a giant drain. Then the boats settled.

We should have all been cheering and slapping high fives and slamming each other on the back. But no one said a thing as we dipped our oars into the waves and rowed back to shore.

CHAPTER 29

AN UNCERTAIN FUTURE

The bonfires still burned on the beaches, and the songs of Walpurgis Night rang through the air. After we pulled the boats into the rental shop and locked them up, Swedish students greeted us with cheers and offered us hot drinks spiced with cinnamon and fruit. My friends and I sat on a log and stared blankly at the roaring flames. The hot drinks helped to stop us from shaking.

Because the fires had been around a bend and out of eyeshot of the swelling wave, no one else knew the danger they'd been in. We were bone weary and our muscles screamed. My guess was that all of us would sleep deeply tonight. And most of us would forget—at least if Blakulla's magic was anything like Grim Hill's.

"What about the witches?" worried Amarjeet. "Are they going to cause us more grief?" She gazed warily at Blakulla, its spiked shape a menacing reminder of our close call.

"You don't have to worry about them for a while," Clive smiled wickedly.

"What did you do?" Jasper looked at him and then at me.

"We've done nothing," I said innocently. We hadn't.

Then to clear it up, Clive said, "Let's just say that right now the witches have their hands full managing a swarm of angry trolls."

Sookie stood on the shore, and I left the comfortable warmth of the bonfire to join her.

"I wanted to be a witch," Sookie turned to me, her eyes on the verge of tears. "It's no fun keeping magic to myself. The witches would let me use all the magic I wanted."

"To do bad things," I reminded her.

Sookie sniffed and wiped her coat sleeve across her nose. "Good things, too."

I stared at her.

"Well," she snuffled, "fun things, at least."

I worried that I'd only delayed the day my sister would become a witch. I now understood that leaving Grim Hill wouldn't save us from magic, nothing would. Our family curse made sure of that. One of us would fight magic, and the other would join the magical realm. That was our fate. But we'd already fought the fates tonight and won. What would our future be?

"Cat, Sookie," Aunt Hildegaard rushed toward us. She was joined by the elderly man we'd met in the café and several other adults their age. "We couldn't rally the young people on the beaches to leave. Then I came back and couldn't find you."

Aunt Hildegaard fiercely hugged the both of us. I was surprised, even though I now understood she'd been trying to protect Sookie since we'd arrived. After all, she'd thought I was the witch.

That night after we'd split up and my friends went back to the hotel, and Sookie was bundled in her bed, I sat down at the pine table in my aunt's kitchen. She'd heated me milk, and I sipped it from the cup. It seemed that nothing, not even the heavy sweater she'd loaned me or the thick quilt across my lap, could keep me warm.

A soft knock rapped on the door. Aunt Hildegaard left the table and cracked open the door as a chill swept into the kitchen. It was Osgaard. I leaped from the table, took the pot of milk on the stove, and went to pour it into his battered cup.

"Your aunt already paid us," said Osgaard. "I'm only here to report the trolls will not work any longer with the witches. The witches lost their new magic when they lost the little girl and won't be bothering the town."

"Consider it a bonus," I said with gratitude, ladling the warm milk into his cup. The trolls had saved my life twice and had taken care of the witches. Okay, some of them had wanted to eat me, but they'd come through in the end.

As Osgaard disappeared into the night, I called after him. "Thank you for everything, Night Roamer."

After I shut the door I asked my aunt, "If the witches' magic didn't last, will my troll magic disappear?"

"I don't know," said Aunt Hildegaard. "I can't say I've ever met anyone who was resuscitated by a troll before."

"What about Sookie?" I couldn't help worry. "Gnawer tricked the witches and didn't ring the bell or light the candle by magic. And Sookie didn't really sign the book. But . . ."

"What?" A shadow crossed my aunt's face.

"Sookie drank some of the witches' brew. That can't be good."

"No, I'm sure it isn't. But again, I've never met someone who managed to defy the witches and lived to tell the tale." My aunt's voice didn't hold back on admiration and her eyes glinted, but only for a moment. "This is new territory for me, and I'm afraid I can't see the future."

"Can anyone?" I remembered how Sookie seemed to see things ahead of time. Also, my own nightmare about falling from the bridge had come true.

My aunt's expression grew uneasy. "Otherworld time stretches out and snaps back as if you are constantly hitting fast-forward and rewind. Sometimes you see shadows of things that may come . . ." My aunt didn't finish. She frowned before she said, "I think you could use a good night's sleep. I'm certain everything will seem much brighter tomorrow."

Aunt Hildegaard had been right. While I wasn't as lucky as most of my friends, who woke up exhausted, thinking they had been to some wild party on Walpurgis Night, the whole night did seem far away and long ago. And Sookie seemed happy hanging out on the farm and playing with the reindeer and other farm animals. For the rest of the trip, my aunt took me into town each day to be with my friends.

When the school closed and the other students transferred, it was clear the other half of the exchange wasn't going to happen. It was for the best, as I couldn't imagine the looks on their faces when they'd discovered we were the oldest students in our school.

For a few blissful moments, we thought we'd be free for fun. Instead, Mr. Morrows and Ms. Dreeble set a killer agenda, and we had to cram science and Viking exhibits into the last days, which left us almost no free time at all. Still, it was hard to complain.

Funny, when I'd first arrived I'd missed home terribly, but now all I could think about was how sad I was to leave.

"Goodbye, dear Cat," my aunt said at the airport. She handed me Sookie's suitcase. "I've spent a good deal of time with your little sister, and she's been calmed by the animals. Remember that. Perhaps you could ask your mother for a pet?"

That wouldn't be an easy sell; Buddy the hamster seemed to stretch Mom's limits. But I promised I'd try.

"Watch over her." My aunt hugged me again.

"*Adjö*," I said, waving goodbye.

I'd do my best with my sister, but would it be good enough? I ushered an uncannily quiet Sookie onto the plane.

"Sit with me, Cat," Zach pointed to the seat beside him. We all had assigned seats, but as soon as we boarded the plane it was a free-for-all.

Clive glowered at Zach and with a sneer sat alone in a row at the back of the plane. I turned and whispered to Jasper, "What's Clive's problem? Zach's always nice to him, so how come Clive is so rude?"

Jasper explained, "Because Clive doesn't like the fact that Zach likes you."

"He does?" I said in surprise.

Jasper shook his head at my woeful ignorance, which was a little harsh considering I'd had other things on my mind these past few weeks.

Now I was faced with two boys with empty seats beside them, both waiting to see who I would choose.

I had dreamed of Zach noticing me since my first day at Darkmont; he was the coolest boy at school. Clive was irritable, impatient, and argumentative, but he'd also jumped off a bridge to save my life.

What happens when your dream becomes reality, and you suddenly aren't sure if it's what you want anymore?

Instead of sitting with either boy, I crammed next to Sookie in the centre aisle with Jasper and Amarjeet.

I had become leery of my dreams coming true.

QUESTIONS FOR DISCUSSION

1. If you could go on a school exchange trip anywhere in the world, where would you go? Don't just think about where you want to go on vacation, but think about a country or city whose culture, history, and people you are interested in learning about.

2. In this book we learn that Cat's family is from Sweden. What culture or cultures are in your family tree?

3. Cat's family doesn't have a lot of money, which makes a lot of activities harder for Cat than for some of her classmates. How do you think this makes Cat feel?

4. What was your first clue that there might be magical forces at work in Sweden?

5. In the book, we learn that trolls are considered bad luck in Sweden. Can you name any things that are considered bad luck in North America or your culture? Why do you think certain things become labelled as bad luck and other things are labelled as good luck?

6. Throughout the book, Cat has a recurring dream that frightens her. Have you ever had a recurring dream? What was it about? Have you ever tried to interpret what your dreams mean?

7. Sookie's magic appears to be getting more and more powerful in every book. What do you think the full expression of Sookie's power will be? In other words, what do you think an adult Sookie will be like? Will she be good or evil, or a mixture of both?

8. Cat observes that Aunt Hildegaard is different from the other ladies her age, like the Greystone sisters. How is she different, and why do you think she might be this way?

9. Cat and Clive started out hating each other back in Book Two, but they appear to be developing a closer bond. Do you think it's possible to start off hating someone and then grow to like them? Do you have any friends who started off as enemies?

10. This book is called *The Family Secret*, and a lot of famous books and stories revolve around families. Do you think your family would make a good subject for a story? Why or why not?

QUESTIONS FOR READING COMPREHENSION

1. Which of Cat's teachers accompany the students to Sweden?

2. Why does Cat's mom send Sookie to Sweden with Cat?

3. Why can't Emily go on the trip to Sweden?

4. What is Cat and Sookie's aunt's name?

5. What grade is Sookie in?

6. What kind of activities do the students do to fund raise for the trip?

7. Why is Cat worried the teachers won't sign her permission form?

8. What does Cat do to convince Ms. Dreeble and Mr. Morrows she is responsible enough to go on the trip?

9. Who comes to see Cat and Sookie off at the airport?

10. Which fairy tale characters does Cat learn about before going to Sweden?

11. What keeps happening in Cat's dreams and nightmares?

12. Why does Sookie need glasses and an eye patch?

13. What happens when Cat and her friends go to collect bottles and cans from around the town?

14. What does Cat's mom make for her when she has to tell Cat that Sookie is going to Sweden with Cat?

15. What kind of seeds does Buddy the hamster eat for dinner?

16. What is Swedish money called?

17. What kind of animal is Sookie hoping will live on their aunt's farm?

18. Why is Sweden called the "land of the midnight sun"?

19. Why does Cat's tour guide seem so annoyed when she meets the group?

20. Where do Cat and Jasper find Sookie after she's disappeared in Stockholm?

21. What figurine does Sookie buy from the shop in Stockholm?

22. What is the name of Darkmont's sister school?

23. What happens to Cat while she is wandering around the fairgrounds with Amarjeet and Jasper?

24. Why are Cat and Sookie so reluctant to go to their aunt's farm?

25. What animal does Sookie try to keep in her aunt's house with her?

26. Who comes to the cabin door for milk every night?

27. What scares Cat when she is bringing milk in from the barn one night?

28. What is a "gymnasieskolan"?

29. What does Clive say is the reason for Cat's aunt's strictness?

30. What does Ms. Grimmaar show the students in Gamla Stan's main square?

31. What festival is going to be celebrated on the lakeshore while the Darkmont students are in town?

32. What reasons does Clive give for thinking something weird is going on in the town?

33. What happens to the Swedish students who are mean to Sookie during a field trip?

34. What swarms everyone during their trip to the lake?

35. What clues Cat, Jasper, and Clive into the fact that Ms. Dreeble and Mr. Morrows are under a spell?

36. What North American celebration is Walpurgis Night compared to?

37. What is "maleficium"?

38. What signs does the old man notice that makes him believe the witches are going to initiate a new member?

39. How can you tell a person is a witch?

40. What is a "familiar"?

41. What is Aunt Hildegaard?

42. Who saves Cat when she falls in the river?

43. Why is Cat able to understand the troll's language?

44. What three items do the witches need to initiate a new witch?

45. Why do the trolls help Cat and her friends trick the witches?

46. How do Cat and her friends get up the mountain to stop the witches' ritual?

47. What do Cat, Jasper, and Clive use to keep the witches away when they recue Sookie?

48. Who saves the kids when the funicular's brakes fail coming down the mountain?

49. What does Cat use to calm down the tidal wave?

50. What reason does Jasper give when Cat wonders why Zach wants to sit with her on the plane?